ON FIRE

On Fire

Dianne Linden

thistledown press

Thistledown Press Ltd.
118 - 20th Street West
Saskatoon, Saskatchewan, S7M 0W6
www.thistledownpress.com

Library and Archives Canada Cataloguing in Publication

Linden, Dianne
On fire / Dianne Linden.

Issued also in electronic format.
ISBN 978-1-927068-38-0

I. Title.

PS8573.I51O5 2013   jC813'.6   C2013-900959-0

Author photograph by Gary Ford
Cover and book design by Jackie Forrie
Printed and bound in Canada

Canada Council   Conseil des Arts   SASKATCHEWAN   Canadian   Patrimoine
for the Arts   du Canada   ARTS BOARD   Heritage   canadien

Thistledown Press gratefully acknowledges the financial assistance of the Canada
Council for the Arts, the Saskatchewan Arts Board, and the Government of Canada
through the Canada Book Fund for its publishing program.

ON FIRE

For my beautiful daughter,
For her beautiful daughter,
And for Adrian Jones, wherever he is

"Some people need a story more than food to stay alive."
— Barry Lopez, *Crow and Weasel*

MATTI

1

TOURETTE'S GIRL

I WAS OUT BEHIND MY HOUSE practicing Karate when I saw him coming down the trail from the Blackstone Wilderness. I thought he was drunk from the way he was weaving back and forth. I picked up a rock because I'm not exactly a black belt yet.

When he got closer, I saw that one of his shoes was gone and his clothes were torn to shreds. Even closer and I noticed he had bruises and cuts everywhere.

I stood there not knowing what to do and then, right in front of me, he collapsed. There was a sound like a hiccup going backwards, several of them and they all came from me. "Get up," I said. "What's wrong with you?"

"On fire," is the answer he gave me. It didn't tell me much. Everything was on fire that summer. Prophet Mountain. Sawtooth Ridge. The Skulls. The Wilderness, especially.

"Get up!" I said again. I pulled on his arm. He just stared at me. His eyes were very blue and something was leaking out of them. I didn't think tears was the right word for it.

"Help!" I yelled. "Somebody," even though I knew when I opened my mouth it was useless. Most of the folks in Blackstone Village had run away from the fires, so there was hardly anyone left to hear me.

Two ravens flew down into a nearby tree and squawked. That was it. There weren't even any dogs left to bark.

I decided to run and get the collapsible wheel chair from our back porch at home. It was for my mom, when she still needed one. "I'll be right back," I told the on-fire guy. "Don't move!" Not that he looked like he was going anywhere.

"Help me," he said.

"I'm going to," I told him. And then I took off, maybe not like I was in the Olympics, but as fast as I could.

I was used to people making fun of me. At school they called me Tourette's Girl, like I came out of a phone booth wearing a costume and made weird noises for their entertainment. But I was a serious person who'd been waiting for a serious purpose.

So what if I couldn't control every little sound that came out of my mouth? So what if I wasn't average? I meant it when I said I'd help this on-fire guy. In fact I meant to save his life.

I hadn't been able to do that for my mom, and I was damned if I'd fail again.

2

JAIL

I TOOK HIM TO WHAT WE called the town office. It was also the fire chief's office, and the mayor's office. And the office of the Justice of the Peace. But I called it *the jail* because a bear broke in one fall trying to get at the apples someone had stored there. After that we got bars on the windows.

We also put in a bed there so people who'd had too many drinks at the Hot Spot Restaurant and Pub could sober up before they drove home.

I knew the jail was empty because almost everyone who hadn't left town earlier was out fire fighting. The door was probably locked, but that wasn't a problem. I'd opened it before with an expired credit card I carry around for things like that.

The name of the fire chief, by the way, and the major and the Justice of the Peace is Frank Iverly. He's my father. I had to grow up fast after we lost my mother and I've called him by his first name ever since.

I almost lost the on-fire guy going over the doorstop. He'd gone to sleep and I had to grab him by the arm at the last minute and get him straight again. Then I opened the door and we went inside. It was hot because the jail had been closed up for a week or so, but I couldn't help that.

"Okay," I said. "You can rest here."

He just looked at me with his leaky eyes.

"This isn't really a jail. You're not under arrest or anything. Lie down. Then I'll go and get help."

He didn't move.

I pushed the chair across the room to where the bed was. "It's comfortable. See?" I patted the mattress. "The bed's a little narrow but it hasn't been slept on by a murderer or anything."

Still nothing.

I shook the chair a little. "Get out," I said.

He went on sitting.

Finally I tipped the chair so far forward that he fell onto the bed face first and stayed there folded over on his side. I straightened out his legs the best I could. "I'm going to get help now," I said again.

Then I ran off to find Marsh Dunegan, who's a friend of ours. I knew he was still around. He was part of the reason Frank let me stay on in the village after he left.

3

EMERGENCY

SOMETHING HAPPENED TO MARSH IN THE war that made him not like being cooped up inside, so he didn't spend much time in a house like other people. I usually tracked him down by watching for his truck.

The day I found the on-fire guy it was parked outside the Hot Spot, which was the only business left open in town, except for the Gas and Grocery. That belonged to Frank and me.

I ran toward the truck and there he was, having a cold one and talking to Allard Grass, the Hot Spot owner. "I've got an emergency," I said. "Come on."

I grabbed Marsh's arm and pulled him up on to his feet. Then I ran ahead, but I could hear his hiking boots crunching on the gravel behind me.

Frank keeps a fan on top of the filing cabinet in the jail. Marsh turned it on when we got back and aimed it at the on-fire guy who was lying in the exact same position I'd left him in. Then Marsh sat down on the side of the bed.

"Hello," he said. Not to me, of course.

"Flying," the on-fire guy said. His face was bright red. It made his eyes look even bluer when he opened them. "Did you see me?"

"Afraid I missed that," Marsh said.

"How I got here," the guy said. "Ravens helped me."

"I brought you here," I said. "Ravens didn't have anything to do with it."

The guy shifted his eyes over to me and shielded them with one hand like he was looking into the light. "Are you an angel?" he asked.

"Of course not," I told him. My face suddenly felt very hot. I went and stood right in front of the fan.

He rolled his head over on the pillow until he was looking at Marsh again. "This isn't heaven then?"

"Far from it," Marsh said. He wrapped his fingers around the on-fire guy's wrist and counted his pulse. "How're you feeling? Still flying?" He stretched the right eye open. Same for the left. "Follow my finger," he said.

The on-fire guy stared at him like his eyelids were locked open in his head. Then slowly, slowly he let them close down.

Marsh opened the only window in the jail and cranked the speed of the fan up as high as it would go. Then he motioned me to follow him outside. "Where'd you find him?" he asked me.

"I was on the Wilderness trail head," I said, "practicing my Karate when I saw him coming down."

"You're sure you've got the direction right?"

"Of course."

Marsh blew out his breath once or twice and looked off somewhere just past my shoulder. Eventually he said, "What are you expecting to do with him?"

"Look after him, obviously," I said. "He asked for my help and he's going to get it."

Marsh smiled in this sad way he has that makes you think you can see his heart in his face. He took off his sunglasses and perched them up on top of his head. Then he rubbed the marks the glasses left on his nose a few times. After that, he went back inside the jail and watched the on-fire guy sleep.

Eventually Marsh rolled him over. There were rows of round, red marks on the backs of his legs. Some of them had scabbed up. Some were weeping clear liquid.

"Are those burns?" I asked.

"Yes," Marsh said. "But not from a wildfire. He's banged up, but he's not burned like that." He slid his glasses back onto his nose. "And I'm pretty sure it isn't because he flew down here."

Marsh got up and motioned me outside again. The bench in front of the town office was in the sun, so we sat on the ground in front of a fir tree. It was still hot there, but the shade at least gave us the idea of coolness.

"We can't keep him here, Matti," Marsh said.

"Why not?"

"He needs to see a doctor."

"You were a medic in the war," I said. I wasn't supposed to mention those days, but I'd seen the medals he kept in the glove compartment of his truck. And Frank told me once that Marsh had saved his life. "Didn't you just give him a checkup?"

"I wouldn't call it that. And my medic certificate isn't up to date."

"Okay," I said. I was trying to think fast. "Then you really don't know what he needs, do you? Professionally speaking, I mean."

Marsh started to comment, but I went right on. "Besides, it's like I said. I'm going to save his life. You ought to understand what that means."

A whole flock of ravens flew down and landed on the roof of the post office. I couldn't remember seeing so many together there before. They bobbed up and down and made little clicking sounds. "Fire's driving them down," Marsh said.

The ravens got louder and louder, like they knew something we should and wanted to get in on the conversation.

"All right. We'll keep him here overnight. I'll park my truck out in front so I can be close by. But after that . . . "

"I could sleep here," I said.

"No, you couldn't." Marsh got up and dusted fir needles off the seat of his shorts. "Cripes, Matti, you're only fourteen. And if he's not better in the morning, I'm driving him down to the hospital in Kingman."

I crossed my arms over my chest.

"I'll also have to get in touch with Frank."

"Good luck with that," I told him.

What Marsh meant was he'd promised to look after me while Frank was gone and he'd have to make sure Frank agreed with what he was doing. That was nothing new.

And what I meant was that out where Frank was fire-fighting, and even most places here in the village for that matter, cell phones and even TVs and computers didn't work very well because we lived in what you call a blackout zone. It would take a few days to get a message through to Frank on Allard's CB radio. Then probably a few more to hear anything back.

Marsh told me to go home and come back around seven, when it was at least a little cooler. "I could just wait here," I said. He told me I couldn't because I didn't know how to wait.

He was wrong about that.

It's true, when I was younger I didn't. I'd stand and stare at the clock in the kitchen until I got a nosebleed, trying to make the hands go faster. But as I got older I understood how time worked.

If I absolutely had to wait I went off somewhere to be alone and blow off a little steam. Sometimes I made sounds like a teakettle when it's boiling. Other times it was more like I was pushing a big rock up a hill or pulling back a hiccup.

Then there were my hands. They were hardly ever still.

I pretended to people that I was practicing sign language when I made shapes with them. But I wasn't signing anything. Just releasing energy.

When you have Tourette's, it can feel really good not to be in control of everything your body does.

4

MRS. STOA

THE OTHER REASON I COULD STAY at home while Frank was away was an old lady named Mrs. Stoa. She was Frank and Marsh's English teacher in high school. They'd brought her down from Riker's Creek at the first of the week when it got too smokey to breathe up there.

She'd made a fuss about leaving, of course. Most of the old-time mountain people did. But now she was here, she seemed to think she owned the place.

I went out on the front porch about five-thirty to kill some time. I like sitting in the swing out there. It helps me stay relaxed. Mrs. Stoa got there before me, though. She's as quiet as a lynx when she wants to be, and tiny compared to me. I'll admit I was a little jealous of that. I've been wearing women's clothes since I was ten.

I'll also admit I'm not very good with the elderly. But I swear I did not mean to sit down on top of her.

"Good Lord, Matilda," she said. She swatted me with a paperback book she was reading and I jumped a mile.

"What are you doing here?" I snapped.

"Reading," she told me. She was wearing a light green surgical mask like we're all supposed to as protection against the smoke in the air.

I thought it looked revolting when she moved her mouth underneath the mask to talk. "Please take that off," I said, "if you're addressing me."

She pushed it up on top of her head like a little green party hat. "What I'm doing is called reading," she said. "You should try it."

I scooted over to the opposite side of the swing. It wasn't the same as being alone and I was nervous about going down to the jail, so I suppose I made a few noises.

"You sound like both sides of a wrestling match," she said. I thought that was pretty harsh.

"I have Tourette's Syndrome, as I'm sure Frank told you. I come out here to be alone and ticoff."

"Who is it you're trying to tick-off, as you say?"

I didn't bother to answer her question.

"A tic," I said, "is like a twitch or a spasm. Some people with T. S. show it in their muscles. I mostly have vocal tics." I didn't mention about my hands. She could figure that out herself.

"As long as you don't start swearing," Mrs. Stoa said. "I draw the line there."

"Most people with Tourette's don't burst out with four-letter words," I told her. "If you don't know any better than that, you should start reading hardcover books that are more educational." She puckered up her lips, but neither of us said anything for a while.

Then I turned and looked at her. "I don't really need you here, you know. I'm okay on my own as long as Marsh is around."

"Your father feels you need someone close by who's better socialized than Marshall." She smoothed out a little wrinkle in her shorts.

I felt like saying, "You missed a few," and pointing at the creases of skin around her knees.

"I won't be here for long, anyway," she said.

"Fine by me," I told her.

"You won't, either." Mrs. Stoa set her book face down in her lap.

"What's that supposed to mean?" I'd just been rocking slowly up to then. After that I tried to go fast enough to make her dizzy, but she was tough.

"It means you need to prepare yourself," she said. "I've lived in these mountains all my life and I've never seen a summer like this one for mean weather."

I gave up trying to swing and stood up.

"Sit down, Matilda." Mrs. Stoa had a stubborn, teacherish kind of look in her eye. That may be why I did what she asked me to.

"What we have between us is called an impasse. You'll never get the best of me and I don't have the energy to get the best of you." She lifted her eyebrows and curved her lips above her chin like she was trying to smile. "So we may as well get along."

"If you stop calling me Matilda and use my real name."

"Which is?"

"Matti Grace Iverly."

"And I suppose you want to be called all three of those names every time I need to talk to you?"

"Matti's enough. But not Matilda."

"Hmmf," Mrs. Stoa said. She went back to her book and started reading out loud. "'*Hey, Crazyred,*' *the crew of Demons*

*cried all together, 'Give him a taste of your claws. Dig him open
a little. Off with his hide.'*

"What are you reading?" I asked her. "R. L. Stine? Aren't you
a little old for that?"

She snapped her head back in my direction. "I was reading
from a paperback called *The Divine Comedy*. The *Inferno*
section. What are they teaching you in school these days?"

"Not that," I said. "We read *Romeo and Juliet* this year in
the eighth grade."

"And?"

"It was okay."

"*The Divine Comedy* was written in the Fourteenth Century
so it's older than Shakespeare. It's about a man named Dante
who travelled through the underworld to save his soul. He
found demons there. And unspeakable horrors."

"What underworld?" I asked.

"Hell," she said. "I imagine you've heard of that?"

"Let me get this straight," I said. "I can say this Dante guy
went through hell without you accusing me of swearing?" I
purred like a cat, entirely for her benefit. You can be creative
with your T.S. if you're willing to make an effort.

"That's correct," Mrs. Stoa said, but I thought she looked
annoyed. "Now why don't you jump up and get us some
lemonade? And don't stint on the sugar."

I took out my credit card and pretended to clean my
fingernails. "I'm tied up right now," I said. "Maybe later."

5

How to Stop a Picnic

I needed to escape from Mrs. Stoa so I was a little early arriving at the jail. Marsh sat on the bench outside reading something — probably a girlie magazine. I 'd found some hidden under the seat of his truck before.

The air was still very hot and the sweat ran down under his ball cap and pooled in his neck. "He's asleep," he said. He folded up whatever he was reading and sat on it.

"Still?"

"Again."

"And that's good?"

"It could be. He was awake long enough to have some chicken soup and crackers and take a walk with me around the room. Then he got back into bed."

"Where'd you get the soup?" I said.

"Allard brought it by from the Hot Spot."

"Allard?" I said. "Is he going to make trouble?"

"He's just interested." Marsh shifted over to cover a corner of the magazine that was showing. "How old do you think this kid is?" he asked.

"Older than me."

"Seventeen or eighteen, I'd guess," Marsh said. "And he's already been through something bad."

"It's called an ordeal, Marsh. You don't have to talk down to me."

"All right. He's been through an ordeal, then. He may come out of it okay, but . . . " Marsh slid his watchband up his arm. It left little dents in his skin and he massaged them for a moment. "We already have a problem."

"Which is?"

"He doesn't know who he is or where — "

I interrupted him. "You mean he has amnesia." That didn't sound like a problem to me. "He'll have to stay here, then, won't he? Because if he doesn't remember where he's from there's nowhere for him to go."

Marsh smiled again the way I described. "How would you feel about running to the Hot Spot before Allard closes and getting me a burger? Or whatever he's got going. I'm starving."

"How would you feel about doing that and I'll stay here?" I said.

"You'll have to promise to stay outside."

"Why? He can barely stand up. Do you think he's dangerous?"

"I don't know what he is, Matti, but you'll have to promise not to go inside."

Standing in the doorway isn't the same as going through the door so I kept my promise. I took a long look at the person I'd rescued. He was sprawled out flat on his back with his legs hanging off the end of the bed because it was too short for him. He could have been dead except I saw his right hand moving up and down on his chest when he breathed.

He looked different already. Marsh had washed the blood and dirt away and put him in a very large t-shirt over what looked like plaid pyjama bottoms cut off at the knees.

He'd washed the on-fire guy's hair and buzzed if off. It made his face look long. And thin. And sort of . . . I'm going to say *helpless*. I don't know if that's the word I want.

I also don't know if it's right to stand and stare at somebody like I was doing. Kind of make a picnic out of it, I mean, when they can't do anything to make you stop.

I guess you have to stop yourself, which is what I did.

And then Marsh came back and sent me home.

6

THE GOLDEN AGE OF SUMMER

IT CLOUDED UP AND COOLED OFF a little just after the on-fire guy came. I think they even got some rain a little higher up. I could actually see across the lake again to the forest and the high, grey mountains on the other side. It was like the Golden Age of Summer had suddenly arrived.

The on-fire guy was well enough the next morning that Marsh said he could stay another day. And another day after that. "But don't get attached," he kept telling me. "We may still have to take him to the hospital."

Marsh was always right outside the door when I came to visit. I sat on a chair beside the bed and talked to the on-fire guy, even though he was usually asleep. I told him my name and quite a bit about myself — how my mother had died right in our house because I couldn't get help there in time and now I just lived with my dad.

How I didn't think there was any question about my intelligence but I still couldn't do certain things at school, like write very well or spell. And how because of my Tourette's, if I made up my mind to go in a certain direction it was very hard for me to change. It almost hurt to do it.

It was easy talking to him since he didn't seem to hear me.

I was just starting to tell him how I treed a kid named Billie Butler in sixth grade for calling me Matti, the Extra-Tourretsial when the guy opened his eyes and looked right at me. "Are you an angel?" he asked me for the second time.

"Of course I'm not," I said. "Cut it out."

He sighed and closed his eyes again. "Then I guess I really am in Hell."

I couldn't understand why he kept mentioning that. Frank always told me hell is something we make for ourselves on earth. It's not a real place, although I know some old people believe it is. Like this mountain man who used to come into town now and then.

One day I came out of school ticcing-off like crazy because I'd spent the whole day trying to hold myself together and be normal and there he was. He pointed at me and said in a raspy voice, "You're possessed! You'll burn like hamburger in the eternal flames and choke on the smoke."

It was just the sort of thing I needed to hear out in public.

"You certainly are not in hell," I told the on-fire guy. "You're in Blackstone Village. We don't usually have fires like this. People come here in the summer to fish and swim. In the fall they hunt and in the winter they heli-ski. If you believe the sign at the edge of town, this is paradise.

"Something happened to my hair," he said. He ran his hands over his scalp.

"It was him." I pointed at Marsh. "Your hair was full of dried blood and worse things. He had to cut it to get it clean."

The guy closed his eyes again. I watched them move back and forth like marbles underneath his eyelids for a while until they finally went still.

7

Visiting Day

Mrs. Stoa didn't think I was making what we had for sale in the Gas and Grocery attractive enough, even though our only customers were guys in forestry trucks or fire fighters. She demonstrated how to make pyramids out of canned baked beans in the front window. The next day she took away the beans — all unsold — and put out corn or tomatoes.

She also made it her mission to clean out our freezer at home. We had a lot of stuff in there people had given us that we didn't want but weren't organized enough to throw away, like bear ham or moose meat chilli.

Every time she whisked something out of the freezer and into the oven, she'd say, "We may as well eat this up. When we evacuate, you'll lose everything that's left." She was still counting on the village burning up even though the weather had changed. "Now let's sit down and enjoy this while we can."

I did sit down at the table with her when she asked me to, usually as a non-eater. Frank may have brought me up to speak my mind. He probably knew he couldn't stop me. But I wasn't supposed to be rude to someone as old as Mrs. Stoa. Unless, of course, I had no alternative.

"I understand you found a young man coming down from the wilderness," she said. I think that was the real reason she wanted us to eat together in the first place. "And now you're looking after him at your father's office."

"Where'd you hear that?" I asked.

"Marsh told me." She slid out of her chair and went to the sink to get a glass of water. She'd given up asking me to bring her things by then, and she got around very well on her own.

"Marsh and I are taking care of him together," I said.

"You should be careful." Mrs. Stoa came back to the table and sat down. "You don't know anything about the boy."

"I know he's practically a man," I said. "Marsh has shaved him twice since he got here."

"Well then," she said. She chased a piece of something suspicious looking across the plate with her fork. "All the more reason for me to meet him."

"You?" I sat back from the table. "It doesn't have anything to do with you."

"Of course it does. Your father asked me to take care of you."

"No, he didn't. He asked you to *stay* here. He asked Marsh to look out for me. Anyway, what use would you be if I really got into trouble? You're too little."

I knew I'd just crossed some kind of rudeness border again, but I couldn't stop myself.

"They say it takes a whole village to raise one child, Matilda," Mrs. Stoa said, "and right now, I'm part of that village." If she couldn't quote her Dante book at me, she'd dig out some old saying like that and wave it in my face.

"He's not a child," I said. "I told you that. And neither am I." I was so upset I had to go outside to tic-off and do the one Karate move I knew over and over.

Marsh said we couldn't ignore Mrs. Stoa's request to come down to the jail, so not long after my meltdown, she made her visitation. She went right inside and had a long look.

The on-fire guy was awake that time and sitting up in bed with a piece of toast. He didn't look at us though, or acknowledge he knew we were there gawking at him like it was parents' day at the zoo.

"I think we should leave him in peace," I said after a while, but Mrs. Stoa wouldn't go. She went right up to him in fact and put her tiny little paw on his shoulder.

It was so light he probably didn't feel it for quite a while. Then when he did make eye contact with her, she sat down and started reading to him. It's not hard to imagine the book she chose.

Marsh and Mrs. Stoa and I went outside after that. "He's going to need care," she told Marsh, like she'd been a nurse for the last century instead of an English teacher. "I don't think she should be alone with him in a closed room."

"She hasn't been," Marsh said.

"Hello," I said. I waved my hand in front of his face. "No need to talk about me like I'm not here."

"And she shouldn't try to take him anywhere."

"Matti?" They both turned and looked at me.

I said, "Okay," like they were expecting me to, but it was a dumb thing to ask me to agree to in the first place. Where would I take him?

All the decent boats in the village marina had been moved farther down toward Kingman. The helicopters up the road at X-Treme Ski would have been fun. But it was a hike up there and anyway, they were all out working in the fire effort.

I suppose we could have looked through all the pamphlets on AIDS and teen-aged pregnancy in the rack at the back of our .

store. Maybe tried out a few elk calls. Or I could have hooked the on-fire guy up to the blood pressure machine. I did that to myself now and then when I was really bored, but I didn't imagine he'd find it entertaining.

After we took Mrs. Stoa home, Marsh said, "The kid might be up to sitting outside for a bit tomorrow since the air is better. Do you think you could find him some clothes?"

"Frank's would be too big," I said, "but I could go to the Thrift Shop. Do you want them A.S.A.P.?"

"Tomorrow will be fine," Marsh said. "He needs everything. But not too early."

I went home right after we talked and got my roller suitcase. I had it packed in case we needed to take off in a hurry, so I emptied it and went to the Thrift Shop in the basement of the Glory Assembly Church.

I didn't have to pick the lock. I knew the key was under the door mat so I used it to let myself in. I wouldn't have broken in anyway. It was a church.

I filled up the suitcase with shirts and shorts and a backpack. I even put in long pants and sweaters for later in the year. I didn't get underwear. I didn't feel right about that. I left an I.O.U. for $20.00 and went home.

My bedroom is on the third floor of the house. I carried the suitcase up the stairs as quietly as I could so Mrs. Stoa wouldn't hear me and want to see everything. After that I sat down on the bed, ticced-off and tried to think of something else to do. I couldn't.

I took the clothes out of the suitcase, refolded them and put them in again.

Then I sat some more.

8

A Second World

I waited as long as I could the next morning, but I still got to the jail with my suitcase before eight o'clock. Marsh was gone somewhere and the on-fire guy was sitting on the bench outside the jail in an old bathrobe, eating peanut butter and toast and drinking a glass of milk.

"Hello," I said. Then my brain conked out. It's harder to talk to someone who's actually awake and listening. "Where's Marsh?"

"He went out to check on something."

"Oh," I said. "I hope you're not going to ask me if I'm an angel again."

The on-fire guy had been looking down at his feet the whole time, like he couldn't believe he actually had two of them. "No." He shook his head. "Why would I do that?"

"I . . . " My face was always turning red around him.. "I'm Matti Iverly. This is Blackstone Village. I live here."

He turned his head to look at me then. "Okay," he said. He moved over on the bench. "You can sit down if you're not afraid of me."

"I'm not afraid," I said. I sat down harder than I meant to. Then I stared off to one side.

"Are you running away from home?" he asked me after a while. He pointed to the suitcase.

"What? Oh," I said. "No. These are clothes for you."

He stuck his bare legs out. They were long and thin and kind of hairy in a golden way. I'm sure he didn't mean for me to notice that. "This bathrobe is a little short," he said.

"You could try the clothes on if you want to. Only not out here." I felt dumb and red again after that.

"Maybe I'll go inside," he said. He was pretty solid standing up, but I had to help him get the suitcase inside.

I waited for him to come back out. Finally I got up to check and he was on the bed asleep again.

"Give him time," Marsh said. He'd finished his errand and was standing behind me. "Come back after lunch."

I did. The sun was out and it was getting warm again. The two of them were sitting on the bench together this time. Marsh had rigged up a beach umbrella to keep the sun off.

The on-fire guy was wearing green shorts and a grey T-shirt with *Blackstone Village Volunteer Fire Dept.* on it. Frank had one like it, but his said Chief, of course.

"Why don't you go for a walk around the building?" Marsh said.

"I thought I couldn't take him anywhere."

"I'll be right here."

When the on-fire guy stood up, I saw that he had a piece of rope tied around his waist to hold the shorts up.

"Maybe go back and get something a little smaller, Matti," Marsh whispered.

"Sorry," I said, but I wasn't apologizing to him.

We walked on a gravel path that went around the building. Marsh couldn't see us when we got on the far side, but we were in the open. We went slowly because the guy was still a little wobbly.

"I need to warn you," I said, just to be on the safe side, "I'm working on my black belt in Karate." I didn't say I had about fifteen years to go.

"Congratulations," the on-fire guy said. Then he sat down on a bench that faced out toward the lake. The water was so smooth that the trees and the mountains and the clouds above them seemed to be floating on top of it. Or else there was a second world just like ours shining up from the bottom of the lake.

"Do you have a cigarette?" he asked me, which ruined the mood.

"I'm fourteen," I said. "I don't smoke."

"I think I might."

"Well, I'm not getting cigarettes for you so don't ask me to." I stood up. "Next thing you know you'll want matches, and anything to do with them, you can count me out. I'm sick of fire."

I didn't tell him how my mother died. I hardly ever talked to people about that.

"Just asking," he said.

We walked back to the jail then. He didn't have a lot to say. He usually didn't. He was kind of mysterious in that way, but I still liked going out with him. I can talk enough for two people when I feel like it.

9

You Don't Know What's Out There

We went out a lot after that. Just short walks to build up the on-fire guy's strength. I tried to ask questions that would jog his memory while we walked. Like he wore a ring on the thumb of his left hand. It was a silver snake with its tail in its mouth. I asked him where he got it.

"I don't know," he said. It was his standard answer.

"Do you think maybe someone gave it to you?" He shrugged, and I should have stopped right there. But I tend to push. It can be a failing of mine.

"Those burn marks on the back of your legs are healing up. How did you get them?"

He ran his hands up and down his legs. "I think it was an accident," he said.

"It wouldn't happen accidentally in rows like that, would it?"

He pushed his hands down deep into the pockets of his shorts. "I don't remember," he said. "Maybe I have enemies."

"What kind of enemies?" I asked.

He turned and looked at me like he was suddenly suspicious. "You don't have any idea what's out there, do you?"

I told Marsh about the conversation later. "Sometimes people burn themselves intentionally," he said.

"Why?"

He didn't try to explain it, and I wouldn't have understood him even if he had. I just couldn't see the on-fire guy doing something like that.

Then I thought of another possibility. "Maybe he wasn't kidding about enemies," I said. "What if someone really did hold him down and do that to him?"

"That would be torture," Marsh said. "And if we find out anything about that, I'll have to get word to the police again."

That gave me a jolt. "What do you mean *again*?" I said.

Marsh began cracking his knuckles, which wasn't a good sign. "When I was down in Kingman yesterday I notified the force that we have an amnesia patient here."

"What?" I whooshed the word out along with quite a lot of air.

"I haven't been able to get in touch with Frank, so I have to guess that's what he'd do."

Pressure started building up in my throat. "You should have asked me first," I said.

"Someone might be looking for him, Matti. Did you think of that? He may have a family somewhere."

I walked away from Marsh and let off steam for quite a while. It's what you're supposed to do when you're trying to control yourself. Then I came back again. "What did the police say? *Is* someone looking for him?"

"Apparently not."

"Well, then," I said.

They asked how old he was. "Probably around eighteen," I told them, "but we can't be sure. They said there are so many displaced people around here right now because of the fires, he'd have to be a lot younger than that before they'd look into it. ."

"So it's up to us to find out who he is and where he's from," I said.

"I'll get Allard to put out a bulletin on his CB radio," Marsh told me. "That might turn up something."

"I suppose," I said.

The police in Kingman weren't the only problem I could see down the road, of course. With the weather getting better, Frank could come home at any time. He wouldn't just sit and wait like Marsh had been doing.

Frank was a detail person. He'd poke around until he knew who the guy was and twenty-eight other things about him. After that I wasn't sure what he'd do.

10

You're Dan Now

I was so preoccupied with my visits to the jail I pretty much forgot bout the Gas and Grocery. Mrs. Stoa didn't, of course. She gave up on her window displays after a few days, but she sat out on the front porch with her book and watched for customers to drive up. I believe that happened once or twice. She phoned up Allard Grass then, and got him to take their money.

She was at her post one morning when I came out with a jug of lemonade and a paper plate of Million Dollar Fudge I'd made the night before. I was beginning to think she had the power to make herself invisible because I didn't even notice her.

"Good morning," she said.

I stopped and whirled around. "What are you doing there?" I tried to hide the fudge behind my back.

"Reading," she said. "As usual. And watching you. I'm supposed to know where you're going."

"I'm going down to the jail," I said. "And I'm sorry, but this food is not for you.

"You call the town office 'the jail'?" she asked.

"Sometimes."

She clucked her tongue. "All that sugar can't be good for the young man. What do you call him, by the way?"

"He still doesn't know his name," I said, "so I don't have a serious one for him."

"Isn't it about time you got one? If he was your pet dog you'd have given him a name by now."

"You just don't understand," I said. Mrs. Stoa had put a stool under the swing to make it easier for her to get up. I pushed it just slightly out of reach with my foot as I went past and out onto the sidewalk.

"You should name him Dante," she called after me. She waved her perfect comedy. "He practically walked out of these pages."

I put that suggestion out of my mind right away.

Marsh's truck was gone when I got to the jail so I knocked on the door. "Breakfast," I called out. I felt like a beautiful waitress in the kind of movie where a stranger comes to town and stays in the hotel she's working in. I wished I'd brought a flower. I wished the flowers hadn't all dried up and were still around to bring.

The on-fire-guy came out in a minute yawning and wearing the volunteer fire department T-shirt, which I'd washed a couple of times already, and some shorts that fit a little better. "Am I too early?" I asked.

He rubbed his face and ran his hands over the stubble on his head. "I guess not, Warden," he said. "Where's the chain gang working today?"

"Whatever that means," I said.

When we were sitting in our usual place looking out over the lake, he took a piece of fudge from the plate and put it in his mouth. His eyes opened really wide. "This is good," he said. "What is it?"

"Million Dollar Fudge," I told him. "It was my mother's recipe." Before he could ask anything about her I changed the subject. "Does it bother you about my T. S.?"

He'd finished his first piece of fudge by then and was licking the chocolate off his fingers. "What is it?"

"Tourette's syndrome. I told you about it when you first got here."

He shook his head and kept on licking. "I don't remember." That bothered me for some reason so I sat and looked at the ravens in the tree above us. There were just a few of them around by then. Most of them had gone.

"You mean the sounds you make?" he asked me.

"That's partly it."

He took more fudge. "Everything has a sound," he said. "Humans. Animals. Sunsets. You wouldn't be normal if you didn't."

"I'm not normal," I said. "Sometimes I feel like I'm a freak."

"No." He took a slurp of lemonade and shook his head. "You're okay."

I laughed, but it came out sharp, almost like a bark. At least the point was turned away from me for once.

I felt more relaxed after that. And even if I didn't like admitting it, Mrs. Stoa was at least partly right about the name situation, so when he'd finished the food, I said, "I think you should have a name."

"What for?"

"Because . . . just let me do this. Pick a letter. Any letter you like and I'll come up with one for you." He didn't react. "Unless you have a better idea. Do you?"

"X," he said.

"What?"

"X is my favourite letter."

"But there aren't any names beginning with X."

"There's Xerox, for one."

"But that's like . . . a business," I said.

He shrugged. He did that a lot and his shoulders were very sharp so I always noticed. "It's still a name. And I like the colour."

I let that pass. "But I mean a serious letter like A. Or B."

"D," he said very quickly.

"That's your letter?"

"Yes."

I tried to think of some D people I knew. "Dwayne," I said. He was someone at school who wasn't too irritating.

"No," the on-fire guy said.

"How about David? He was a giant killer."

"I think that was Jack," he said, "but no, anyway." He wouldn't give a reason.

After that I thought about names from the comics. "Donald?" I said. "Daffy? Or Dick?" No to all of them. "Darren?" That was another name from school.

"Wait," he said. "I think I should have picked R for Rumpelstiltskin." He pointed his finger at me. "Since you haven't guessed it, you'll have to give me your first born child." He laughed.

I turned my back to him. "I'm not having children," I said. "They might turn out like me." I didn't talk for a while after that.

"Just leave it," he said finally. I don't want a name."

I was on a roll though, and like I said it isn't easy for me to stop when that happens. A name popped out of my mouth like it had been waiting there all the time. "How about Dante?" I said. He got a puzzled look on his face. "Or it could be Dan for short."

"Dante went through hell, didn't he?"

"You've heard about him?"

"Read about him, probably."

"Where?"

"I don't know. Maybe it was a computer game. I just remember it was a long story. And not the kind of thing you'd discuss with a kid."

"I'm not a kid," I said. "What was it about?"

He rubbed his eyes. "Torture. People get cut open and eaten alive so . . . there's also cannibalism. Monsters." He hesitated. "Demons. It's all red." Then he suddenly snapped at me. "I don't want to talk about it."

"I was just trying to help," I said. "You asked me to." I went over and sat on the ground away from him.

After a while, he came and stood behind me. "Look," he said. "All I have inside my head right now is blue. Blue is true. I want it to stay that way."

"Blue? What do you mean?"

"B-looo," he said, like making two syllables instead of one would get his point across.

"I know my colours," I told him. "But what are you talking about?"

"I'm talking about your questions," he said. "You have to stop asking them."

I tried to be what you call light-hearted after that because I could see he was getting agitated. "I guess it's no to Dante then," I said.

"I can live with X," he said.

"I can't."

I wasn't about to go around referring to the person whose life I was trying to save with a single letter of the alphabet. It was insulting to both of us.

"If you don't want a name," I told him, "I can't do anything about that. But in my head you're going to be Dan. I'm afraid that's the best I can do."

11

VIRGIL

DAN AND I STARTED TAKING LONGER walks down to the lake after that. We used the path that dips down behind of the jail. This time of year the water should have been full of kids yelling and thrashing their way out to the float.

And our little sand beach should have had blankets and sunbathers and gum wrappers and coke cans and ghetto blasters all over it. But even with better weather and a few people trickling back into town, it was empty.

I spread out the blanket I'd brought and we sat there for a while watching helicopters fly over with their belly buckets full of water. Dan pointed across the lake. "Do people live over there?" he asked.

"A few," I said. "There used to be a lead mine there. And a town called Cato City. It's pretty much a ghost town now."

"Are they friendly ghosts?"

"What?" I said. Sometimes I worried about the way he talked. Maybe I didn't worry enough.

"I was just wondering if you ever went over there."

"Not too often. There's nothing to see but fallen down buildings."

"I thought you said there were a few people there."

"Well, actually just a girl I sort of know from school. She's a year older and doesn't have much to do with me, of course. Her name's Bee Laverdiere. Her hair's black and long. She's very beautiful."

"She lives there by herself in a house that's falling down?"

"I suppose her house is okay," I said, "but she's probably alone a lot. Her mother goes away to cook for hunting camps and stuff like that. I've heard Bee has a younger sister, too. Then there's her cousin Virgil. He's what you call a guide."

"What kind?"

"Hunters, mostly. He takes them back into the mountains to fish or find bear or elk or mountain lions. He's gone now, if you're wondering. The whole family's been evacuated."

That was a lie. The fire wasn't even supposed to get to Cato City. They'd burned off a huge section of forest up at the lake head. And Blackstone Lake itself is too wide for any fire to jump, except maybe at the end of the world.

I wasn't interested in having Dan meet Bee, though. He'd probably fall in love with her like all the other boys in school. For all I knew she could also fall in love with him, like in *Romeo and Juliet*. Then where would that leave me?

While we sat there we saw a black speck moving toward us out on the water. I thought it was a couple of ravens floating on a dead head at first. Then it got closer and I could make out the outline of a boat. "Oh crap," I thought. "That's probably Bee now."

It was her cousin Virgil, though. Big boats go into the marina at the north end of the village, but we have a dock on the edge of the beach where small boats can tie up. He was making for that.

He cut the kicker, which is what we call an out-board motor, and paddled the last distance into shore. I got up and held out my hand so he could throw the guide rope to me. "Hello, Virgil," I said.

"Who are you again?" he asked.

"Matti Iverly. I know your cousin, Bee. She didn't come with you?"

Virgil climbed out of the boat all in one smooth motion. He took the rope from me and tied up. "Bee and Charlene went to our Grandma's in Kingman," he said. "And my aunt's cooking for tree planters, so there's nobody there but me." His eyes were amber coloured and his hair was long and dark like Bee's.

"This is my friend," I said. "He has amnesia. Do you think we could borrow your boat?"

"Have you got a license?" Virgil asked.

"I'm not old enough."

"What about him?" He looked at Dan.

"Probably not," Dan said.

Virgil dipped his red bandana into the lake. He wrung it out and tied it around his head. "I'll have to say no, then, Marti. I've only got one life jacket and it's for my little cousin Charlene. What if one of you drowns?"

"It's Matti," I said. "And we won't."

Virgil went on like he hadn't heard me. "The government doesn't like people drowning without a license."

"I'm a good swimmer," I told him. I guess I was showing off for Dan. "I've been out on this lake all my life. I could probably swim across it if I had to."

"Oh, yeah?" Virgil said. "How about your friend?" Dan shrugged. "I'd suggest we throw him into the lake and find out. But I've got my good clothes on. If I have to jump in and rescue him, I'll get them wet."

He was wearing black jeans, a T-shirt and a vest, if that's what you call good. "Come on, Virgil," I said. "Please."

"Afraid not." He began to walk up the path to town. "Don't take my boat, okay?" he called over his shoulder. "I'm just here to see if any of my girlfriends are back. I don't know how long I'm staying."

"They aren't," I called after him. Virgil stopped and turned around.

"It's a pretty long list. You sure you know them all?"

"Maybe not," I said. He walked away again. This time he didn't come back.

12

STORIES

AT SUPPER MRS. STOA WANTED TO know if I'd used her idea and given *that young man,* as she called him, a name. "He doesn't want a name." I said. "He told me to call him X."

"You can't do that," she said. "He's a human being."

For once we agreed on something. "I told him I'd call him Dan."

"It's definitely his story."

"I didn't pick it because of what you said. I . . . it just . . . came out."

"Ah," Mrs. Stoa said. She'd emptied out all the old stuff she'd found in the freezer and now she was serving a tuna casserole she'd made herself. She pushed the dish over toward me. I lifted some melted cheese off the top.

"Do you honestly think," I asked her, "that a story from hundreds of years ago can pop up in somebody's life like a chipmunk out of a pile of rocks and take it over?"

"Don't pick at the topping," she said. "Put some on your plate."

I did. The peas in it were mushy, like they came out of a can, but otherwise it had no taste, which was an improvement.

"You're very literal, Matilda," she said. "And you're missing the point." When she smiled I could see a pea skin stuck in between her teeth.

"What is the point?" I asked her.

"These old stories don't take us over as you're suggesting. But they are in the world. And sometimes we grab onto them."

"Dan wasn't even thinking about your Dante story until I mentioned it to him," I said.

"But he is thinking about it now. And so are you."

While we were clearing off the dishes, I asked her, just casually so she wouldn't think I was at all interested, "How did Dante get through hell, if you'll pardon my French? If it was as bad as you said."

"Oh, it was bad. The horrors were endless."

"So? How did he survive all alone like that?"

"He wasn't alone," Mrs. Stoa said. She fixed herself a glass of lemonade and dropped in a maraschino cherry. "He had the ghost of the poet Virgil with him as his guide for part of the way. And he had Beatrice, his soul mate. He was also met by . . . "

"That's enough information," I said. I stuck my fingers in my ears and hummed.

I didn't know anyone named Beatrice. I did know a girl named Bee. And we did have a kind of guide living in the area. He was so outdoorsy I doubted if he'd ever even been in a library, so he wasn't a poet. And he certainly wasn't dead. But his name was Virgil and I'd recently introduced him to Dan.

I remembered Dan telling me there was torture involved in Dante's book. "Endless horrors," Mrs. Stoa'd said. I had no intention of latching on to a story like that. And I didn't want it latching on to me.

13

Hyperventilation

Just as I was leaving one morning to go down to the jail, Marsh pulled up in front of our house in his truck. He rolled down the window and called to me. "Could you get in, Matti?" he said. "I need to talk to you."

We sat for a while and watched a family who had just come back to town unload their luggage. They let their yappy little dog out of the car and he ran around barking. Then he had a pee on the front lawn, which meant, I think, "Ah! Home at last."

I needed to get on with my day though so I asked, "What did you want, Marsh?"

He took a big breath. Then he turned and smiled at me.

I had a theory about Marsh's smile. I think he was in love with somebody once. I don't know if they were married or had kids. But even when he was in the war his heart lit up like a hundred-watt bulb whenever he thought of her, which was most of the time.

Then he came home and something happened. She died, maybe or left.

After that, his heart pretty much went out. It's just that at certain times like when he smiles his body remembers how he used to feel. But it also remembers he doesn't feel that way any more. That's where the sadness comes from.

"Allard got a message from Frank last night," Marsh said. "He's hoping to get home in the next few days."

"Good," I said, even though I knew there would be complications. "Did you explain to him about Dan?"

"Who?"

"That's what I call the person who's living in the town office."

"Oh," Marsh said, but he didn't look at me when he said it. "I told him."

"And did you also tell him Dan's getting better every day and we're taking good care of him?"

"I did," Marsh said.

"What did Frank think about that?"

"He thinks it's good you found him and he knows you're doing your absolute best."

Just the way he picked his way through what he was saying — carefully, like he was walking barefoot over gravel, I knew there was a *but* coming. I said it for him. "But?"

Marsh began cracking his knuckles. "He also thinks it's time to take the boy down to Kingman."

"No," I said. "The police don't want him. Did you tell Frank that?"

"I did, Matti, but look," Marsh said, although he wasn't looking at me. Just cracking his knuckles and staring straight ahead. "He's been here over a week and — "

"It hasn't been that long."

"It has. I told you when he came that we might not be able to keep him here."

"Well, it isn't just Frank's decision to make, is it?" I opened the door of the truck. "Or yours. And anyway, Dan's starting to remember things. Like he remembers reading about a guy called Dante. I'm working with him and he'll remember other stuff. You just have to give me time." I kept speeding up until I was gasping for breath. *Hyperventilation*, it's called.

"That's general knowledge, Matti," Marsh said. He finally turned and looked at me. His face was all droopy and hang-dog. "It's nothing to do with him personally. Does he remember his name? Or where he lived?"

"Not yet. I don't think he wants to."

"Matti." Marsh pushed his hands toward his knees like he was holding something down. "I know this is hard, but you have to be reasonable."

"No!" I shouted, and then I had a real meltdown. "I won't be." I got out of the truck and slammed the door. "Frank thinks Dan's crazy, doesn't he? He wants to send him to the Mental Hospital in Metal Springs because you repeated the stuff Dan said about flying.

"But he doesn't talk about flying anymore. And he's not crazy!" I opened the door and slammed it shut again. "And I won't let either of you take him anywhere!"

I ran away from Marsh and kept going until I was on the path to the Blackstone Wilderness where I first met Dan. When the trail began to climb I slowed down and walked. When I was too out of breath to even do that anymore, I sat down behind a boulder and cried and ticced-off.

I wanted to be hidden in case Marsh came looking for me. He didn't. But when I finally calmed down again and got back to the trailhead, he was waiting there.

"Frank doesn't think the kid's crazy," he said. "And I don't either. We don't use words like that. But Frank does think he needs help that we can't give him here, and I have to say I agree."

I glared at Marsh and didn't answer back.

"And he won't necessarily go to the Metal Springs hospital. We'll try the General first. You can come with us to see where he's going to stay."

Marsh took hold of my arm but I shook him off and began to walk away. "When are you going?" I asked. I needed to know that so I could make plans.

"Not today." Marsh walked along beside me. "Frank won't be back that soon." I slowed down then so I could pay attention to what he was saying. "Tomorrow if he gets here early enough. The next day for sure."

Finally I stopped. "The day after tomorrow would be better," I said. Marsh agreed. I think he was relieved because it looked like I was being sensible.

I wasn't. I'd heard Frank talking about what they did to people like Dan at Metal Springs. Someone he knew went there. They tied the guy down on a table and shot his brain full of electricity. In my book that's torture.

Marsh said if we found out Dan had been tortured we'd have to call the police. Now he and Frank were taking him some place where it could happen again. I was so angry I was beside myself. I think that's an expression I've heard.

Like there was me, Matti Iverly, glaring at Marsh. And another Matti was standing shoulder to shoulder with her. The second one was invisible. And she was howling bloody murder.

14

The End of the Golden Age

ALL I COULD THINK ABOUT AFTER that was getting Dan away. And the only place far enough was Cato City across the lake. We might run into Virgil there, but he went his own way and didn't stick his nose in other people's business. Everyone else was gone.

There had to be some decent buildings in Cato City. Bee lived there. Her house would be empty for a while, if I could find it.

Or I'd take our tent. Frank wouldn't even notice it was missing. I could get some food over there, too, if I just found a way to move everything.

I went down to the big marina to see if any decent boats were back. All I found was a leaky rowboat. I could try getting supplies across in it. I'd have to bail like crazy but I'd manage.

Then I'd need to get Dan across. I was pretty sure I could find a life jacket for him somewhere. I'd break into a couple of houses if I had to.

By the time I got to the jail, the sun was pretty high in the sky. Dan was outside on the bench, yawning. His eyes looked red and watery.

"Sorry I'm late," I said. "Are you okay?"

"I didn't sleep much."

"Sorry," I said again. "Did you have anything to eat?"

"Marsh came by."

"Oh? Did he say anything?"

"'Hi. Good bye.' In between he said 'How are you.'" Dan's voice was all on one level when he talked. Monotone.

"Anything else?"

"No. And I don't want to play Twenty Questions."

That was crabby, I thought, but he'd been crabby a few times before, usually when he needed to eat. I didn't take it to mean anything.

I suggested we go to the Hot Spot for something. If it was breaking one of the rules I was supposed to live by, I didn't care. I wasn't playing by those rules anymore.

When we got to the Hot Spot and Dan was sitting down, I went to the counter and ordered cokes and fries with ketchup for both of us. "I don't have any cash with me," I told Allard. "I have some at home so I'm good for it."

"You want to put it on Frank's tab with all the rest of the kid's food?" he asked.

"Please," I said.

Another thing for Frank to get excited about.

Allard brought the food over to the table when it was ready. He tried to talk to Dan but he didn't have any better luck than I did. After a while, he went back behind the counter.

Dan put a load of salt and ketchup on the fries. Then he just looked at them. "Try one," I said.

He did. And he grunted, like they were good. I thought he'd get a rhythm going and try another one, but that didn't happen.

A bunch of firefighters in their yellow suits came into the Hot Spot while we were there. They were laughing and talking loud — taking a break and having fun for a change.

They seemed friendly enough but when Dan saw them he scraped back from the table and stood up so fast the chair fell over backward.

"What is it?" I asked him. I stood up, too.

"Problem?" one of the firefighters said. He looked over at Dan. The way I saw it, he was just acting concerned.

Allard came over and stood beside me. "Something wrong with the food?" he asked.

"You told them where I was," Dan hissed at me. He backed away from the fire fighters. When he got to the door, he turned and ran outside.

"Slow down," I called after him. "Tell me what's wrong." I followed him until we got back to the jail.

"I've seen them before," he said. "They're demons." His eyes moved back and forth like he was watching a speeded up movie. "They hid in the smoke. Then they chased me and set the world on fire."

I had to think for a minute before I figured out what he was talking about. "They're firefighters," I said. You probably saw some when you were lost and confused. You were lost out there, weren't you?"

"You've ruined everything," Dan said. He gave me a look that stabbed right into my heart. Then he went inside and closed the door. I heard him locking it.

"I don't understand," I called after him. "I haven't told anybody!" I was blubbering so much I had to wipe my nose on the hem of my shirt.

I waited for what felt like hours. Allard came out to check on us a couple of times. Marsh knocked on the door. But Dan wouldn't come out.

The sun was down behind the mountains when I got home. Crickets were making their raspy music, which I usually liked. Now it made me think of metal sawing away at dry bones.

That was the end of the Golden Age.

15

GONE

I GOT UP VERY EARLY THE next morning. I found the tent out in the garage and an old life jacket. I hid them in the bushes and bracken of the house next door. When I poked around for a bailing pail, I also found an inflatable rubber raft. It was heavy but I got it into the bushes as well.

My plan was to move everything over to Cato City that night, including whatever canned food I could get away with. Then early the next morning I'd get Dan and we'd be gone.

Because of all that activity, I got to the jail house a little later than usual. Dan wasn't sitting outside and the door was closed. I waited for a while trying to decide if I should go home and give him some more space for a few hours.

Marsh drove up in his truck and got out while I was waiting. "Matti," he said. His face was all pulled together.

"You're not taking him to the hospital now," I said. "Frank isn't here and I need another day."

"We've run out of time," Marsh said.

"What are you talking about?"

He swallowed hard. "Dan's gone."

"What do you mean?"

Marsh pointed to the jail. "It's empty," he said.

I tried the door. It wasn't locked anymore. The bed was made and very neat, but Dan wasn't there.

I ran back outside. "I said I needed time," I yelled. "And you said I could go with him." I hit Marsh very hard in the chest with my fists. Once. Twice. Three times.

He took hold of my fists and held them tight.

"I didn't take him anywhere, Matti," he said. "He left. He was gone when I checked on him at six-thirty this morning."

"I don't believe you."

"It's the truth. He's not here anymore. He's gone."

"But he can't be," I wailed. "I had plans."

Marsh shook his head. "He took everything and left. I've driven half way down toward Kingman and I can't find him. I'm very sorry Matti, but he's gone."

16

One Less Crazy Person

Blackstone Village is small but there are lots of places where you can disappear. I searched and Dan wasn't in any of the ones I knew about. I considered that maybe he was thinking what I was thinking and he'd already gone across to Cato City so I went down to the beach.

The sand was chewed up by the dock like a person had been there. Maybe two people. But that could have been from birds. Or rabbits. Or a dog someone had brought back with them. It didn't mean anything.

What did mean something, I thought, was finding Dan's silver ring shining up from the sand at the water's edge. I picked it up. Why would he have left it there unless he wanted to leave me a clue?

Maybe he wanted me to know he was swimming across. He wasn't that strong yet, but he might have been able to make it.

Even at the time I was thinking that though, I knew it was mostly a wish. I held on to it for a while, the way you do when you don't want to see how things really are, but underneath I was afraid he'd started to swim across to the other side, but couldn't get there.

Or worse, maybe he'd just gone out into the water and hadn't even tried to swim. That meant he'd left the ring to say goodbye.

Think about it. Something so bad had happened to him that he'd forgotten who he was. Then he saw those guys in yellow and they terrified him. Maybe when he was lost out in the fire area, fire fighters really did attack him. They could have held him down and burned him. How do I know what guys get up to out in the wilderness?

Being lost and confused and tortured would be enough to make most people want to drown themselves. I even thought about it myself while I was sitting there.

I promised to save Dan's life. I tried, but I failed him. Just like I failed my mother.

I wanted to walk into the lake and disappear.

When I finally left the beach I decided not to tell anybody what I'd found out. Marsh said he and Frank didn't use words like *crazy* or *lunatic*. And I didn't think Mrs. Stoa would. But some people in town might.

I could just imagine what they'd say. "Did you hear about that lost kid who ended up in the lake? One less crazy person in the world."

I couldn't stand to think of people talking that way about Dan. It's bad enough to be confused and screwed up. You shouldn't be blamed for it.

17

CONFLAGRATION

I STAYED IN MY ROOM THE rest of the day with the door locked. I got a chain out of my dresser drawer and put Dan's ring on it. Then I hung it around my neck. After that I laid down on the bed and stared out the window.

I don't think I noticed the wind coming up at first. When I finally did, I didn't pay any attention. What did I care about the weather? Dan was dead.

It seemed like I heard Marsh's voice through the floor boards for a while. And there were steps on the stairs. Sometimes heavy. Sometimes light. And lots of knocking which I didn't answer.

It got dark while I was lying there. Somewhere in my brain I was aware that it was pretty early for that. Lightning flashed a few times. There was thunder. I basically ignored it all — rolled over and zombied-out.

The next thing I knew Mrs. Stoa was rapping on the door. And not so quietly this time. "Matilda!" she called. "Open the door. I need to talk to you." I pulled the pillow over my head and didn't answer.

"It's serious. Open this door at once!"

I threw the pillow on the floor. "What will you do if I don't?" I shouted. "Force your way in?" I actually had to laugh, thinking about Mrs. Stoa with her little bird bones trying to break down my door.

"There's a new fire, Matti." Now it was Marsh talking. And he was using what I imagined was his war voice. "We have evacuation orders. Open up!"

I unlocked the door and opened it just a crack. "I don't want to talk to you," I said. But to be honest I lost most of my steam when I saw Marsh's face. It looked like it was carved out of stone.

He and Mrs. Stoa were both standing in the hall holding flashlights. That's when I understood that the electricity was off in the house. "We don't have time for this now," Marsh said. "They've had lightning strikes up on Devil's Thumb and the wind's blowing the fire this way fast.

"Get your suitcase and come down stairs. That's an order."

By the time I'd done that, and I was pretty quick, Mrs. Stoa was sitting on the living room couch wearing her green mask. Her suitcase was on the floor beside her. "Marshall is making one last check before we leave," she said.

She kept the mask on to talk and I didn't comment about it. I stood with my back toward her and watched out the front window. I could barely see across the street for the smoke.

"So it's finally here," she said.

I started counting breaths. About every fourth or fifth, I felt a little catch in my throat.

"It's here," she said again. This time a little louder.

I whirled around. "Listen, Mrs. Stoa. This is a very hard time for me, and I don't want to hear anything from you about the end of the world. As far as I'm concerned, it's already happened anyway."

"I never said the world was ending," she told me. "I said conflagration was coming. A great fire."

"That's close enough."

"It's happened before. We'll survive. We're mountain people."

I turned away from her and looked out the window again. I was in the process of taking back what I'd thought about not caring if we burned up, when I saw two orange lights like eyes coming through the haze.

I thought at first it was Marsh, but it was an army truck filled with firefighters. It went past. Then another. And another.

After that a jeep with a revolving light on the top came by from the opposite direction and stopped in front of our house. A guy in some kind of uniform got out and started up the front walk. I opened the door.

It was like we were in a movie — everything slow and lazy except my heart, which was beating like a stopwatch. "Anyone in the house who needs help getting out?" the guy asked me.

"It's all right," Marsh said. He'd pulled up behind the guy in the uniform and came running up onto the porch. "We're leaving."

18

D for Dead

I'D EXPECTED MRS. STOA TO RIDE in the front of the truck with Marsh, but she got in the back of the extended cab beside me. After we'd gone through a couple of roadblocks, she turned to me and whispered, "I know you're worried about Dan, but he'll come through."

"Like your guy Dante, I guess you mean," I said. "But you've got the wrong *D* word."

I wanted her to leave me alone so I told her flat out what I believed. It didn't matter that I'd said I wasn't going to. I didn't see myself then as a person who kept her word.

"Not D for Dante," I told her. "D for Dead. He drowned in the lake."

"I don't believe it," she said. "Do you have any proof?"

I showed her the ring, which I still had on a chain around my neck. "He always wore this. I found it by the water's edge."

Mrs. Stoa shook her head. "Rings get lost. But he won't. He'll live."

I wanted to believe what she was saying, but all she had to go on was an old story. What was it called, anyway? *The Divine Comedy*? So far I wasn't laughing.

DAN

1

Nothing Can Track
A Human over Water

He opens the door of the town office and looks out cautiously. The sky in the east is humming with colour but it's already hot. And the air is hushed. In all of creation he thinks he may be the only one awake.

Except for the ravens. Two of them fly down and settle in the fir tree nearby. They cock their heads and look at him. Bob up and down and click their thick beaks. They want him to go. Now that the demons know where he is, it isn't safe to stay.

He stuffs his clothes into the backpack, walks out and closes the door behind him. When he reaches the lake, he squats down and dips his hands in the water, sluicing some of it on his face and up over the back of his neck.

The snake ring slips off his thumb and sinks down into the sand. He starts to reach for it, then straightens up when he feels the shadow of something behind him.

He turns and looks into eyes that are level with his and rimmed with darkness. "You're the amnesia guy," the mouth below the eyes says." Do you have another name to go with that yet?"

Dan shakes his head.

"I'm Virgil." There follows the whisper of a handshake. "I guess you remember meeting me the other day with what's her name. Frank Iverly's girl?"

Dan doesn't answer.

They size each other up, although Virgil does most of the sizing. "Okay," he says. He nods a few times as if he's made up his mind about something. "Have a good one." He turns and walks toward his boat.

"Wait!" Dan is trying to remember something. "You're . . . a guide, aren't you?"

Virgil stops and turns around. "You need one?"

"I might." Dan points across the lake. "What's over there?"

"Cato City? History, mostly. Mine tailings. Lots of rotten wood. Buildings falling down. A few still standing, like the ones me and my relatives live in. Why? You want to go over there?"

"Maybe. What about people?"

"Everybody's gone for the summer except me," Virgil says. "And I'm about to leave myself." He turns toward his boat again. "Make up your mind if you're coming. I've been up all night . . . checking on things in town. I just need to get a little sleep at home and pack up before I leave for Kingman."

While they're launching the boat, Virgil gestures toward the two ravens who've settled on a rock at the water's edge. "You three together?"

"They follow me around," Dan says.

"We have quite a few ravens here, especially this summer. You sure they're always the same ones?"

"They tell me they saved my life."

"Oh, yeah?" Virgil steadies the boat while Dan climbs in. "Ravens told you that?" He gets into the boat next. "Of course ravens are known to exaggerate."

Virgil picks up a paddle and holds it above the water while he thinks. "Two of them together means something, though." He knifes the paddle down through the water and pushes away from him. The boat moves out into the lake.

"What?" Dan asks.

Virgil shakes his head. "I'm kind of like you." He drops the paddle on the floor of the boat. "There's a lot of stuff I can't remember. Better hold on," he says as he starts up the kicker. "This is a powerful motor."

"Two stroke?" Dan asks.

"You know about motors?" Virgil asks.

"I know about how they sound. What's your horse power?"

"Where I come from we say moose power. About five." Virgil watches Dan as they move slowly out into the water. It's possible he winks, although it may be the breeze off their passage catching in his eye.

The sun is well up by now, the surface of the lake brilliant with only a swirl of motion underneath. Virgil points to the long, wispy cloud trails above them. "There's your horses," he says. "Mare's tails. Means a change in the weather."

Dan follows the sweep of Virgil's arm with his eyes. Then looks back down at the water. "How deep is it here?" he asks.

"Don't know," Virgil says. "Never been to the bottom before." He motions toward the life jacket crumpled on the floor of the boat. "It's for my little cousin Charlene. You ever meet her?"

"No."

"It's just as well. She's a holy terror. Anyway, that jacket won't fit you, but you feel free to grab a hold of it if we go under." He adjusts the throttle and they pick up speed.

Nothing can track a human over water. Does Virgil say that? Or is it the lake itself reassuring Dan? He stares at its shining surface. He'd like to travel in Virgil's boat forever and let the world slip quietly by.

2

Sleep

THERE ARE STEEP WHITE BLUFFS ON the Cato City side of the lake. They're streaked with black in places. And with rusty brown. Virgil turns the boat and moves it parallel to them until a break suddenly opens up in the rock.

He guides the boat through that and into a sheltered harbour with a beach of black and tan pebbles. He ties up to a float made out of deadheads chained together, takes off his shoes and holds them over his head. Then he slips into water that rises up to his ribs.

"Isn't there any easier way?" Dan calls after him.

"Sure," Virgil calls back. "A bit farther north we built a pretty solid dock. But this is the one I use. People I bring here to fish want to feel like they're getting the real thing."

He stops and turns. "It's a hot day. Water feels good. You don't expect me to carry you, I hope?"

"No."

"Because you can sit in my boat all day if you want to. But if you're still here when I wake up, you'll have to go down to Kingman with me." Virgil puts his shoes on again and begins to climb a steep path sheltered from the lake by aspen and lodge pole pine.

"What's in Kingman?" Dan calls.

"People." Virgil's voice comes out of the trees. "Supplies. Nothing burning." He continues to climb and soon he's out of sight.

By the time Dan gets to the shore he's exhausted. He picks a grassy area sheltered by a dense stand of trees and lies down. He hears waves lapping quietly at the rocks on the shore. Lichen crumbling those rocks into sand. Ravens and nuthatches announce the passing of time before he closes his eyes and drifts into silence.

The sun is far in the west when he opens his eyes again. It takes him a moment to establish where he is. Then he stands up and stretches his long spine.

The wind has picked up. He walks out from the cover of the trees and feels how it's scuffing up the surface of the lake. The sky has changed, too.

It's all clouds now and there's a darker charcoal smudge like a giant thumbprint moving over the mountains on the other side. It becomes a fist, and then while he watches, opens out into a hand groping toward him.

An omen, he thinks. It may not be safe here after all. Maybe he should go with Virgil to Kingman and then slip away.

He walks back toward the float and stands looking at it for quite a while before he puts words to what's wrong.

The boat is gone.

Virgil has left without him.

3

The Dead Are Always with Us

DAN OFTEN HAS TO STOP AND get his breath as he climbs the steep path up from the lake. To his left he begins to see piles of decaying wood, and then further on, the broken bones of houses. Here and there a stone chimney or the skeleton of a roof survives. All around he hears a mournful sighing.

When he finally finds an A-frame with its roof on tight, he mounts the steps to the front deck. The door is locked. He knocks. Rattles the handle. He even shoves his shoulder against the door, but nothing responds except a few aspen leaves, withered from the drought. They drop to the ground and the wind eddies them around his feet.

There are two Adirondack chairs on the deck. He sets his pack down and sits in one of them. He can see all the way down to the lake and across to the nightmare on the other side. Lightning flashes. He counts to five before he hears the following thunder.

He leaves the chair then. Moves to the floor in front of the deck railing and hunches his back against what's happening across the water.

The sky grows dusky while he huddles there. What's left of the sun shows blood red. The wind increases, tearing at the trees and flinging branches down around him, but his hearing is so acute he's still able to detect someone breathing up behind him.

It's quiet breathing — the soft inhale and exhale of a sleepwalker sneaking up on his dreams. He turns and sees Virgil holding a flashlight in his hand. "When did you come back?" Dan asks.

"I never left," Virgil says. "Why don't you go inside?"

"The door's locked."

"Of course. It's private property." Virgil's light moves around to the side door of the cabin and Dan follows. "People usually hide a key under their door mat," Virgil tells him. "You take it and open the door."

Dan bends over to look, but there's no key there.

"Or," Virgil says, pointing at a pane of glass in the door, "you break this and let yourself in. Careful, though. Wrap something around your arm so you won't be cut."

Dan takes a T-shirt out of his back pack and uses it for protection. One tap and his arm is through.

There's food in the cupboards: pork and beans. Tuna fish. Vegetable soup. Their labels glow in the murky light. "Get a can opener and help yourself," Virgil says. He shows Dan where to look.

The power is turned off so Dan eats the beans cold — goes on eating until he can't make any more go down. Then he unlocks the front door and goes out to where Virgil is standing on the deck. It's dark as pitch outside now and the lake has turned to fire. He hears the forces of nature all around him.

"Are you afraid of the dead?" Virgil asks.

"Why?"

"Take a look." Virgil holds up the flashlight and Dan sees that they're everywhere — roosting up in the trees. Sitting on the deck railing.On the stairs.On the rocks beyond that. And more are coming.

They're riding on horseback or in carriages and mining cars. Or they're walking. Sometimes carrying each other. Sometimes crawling. They're even rappelling down from the steep cliff behind the cabin.

There are thousands of them, all the colour of cobwebs.

"Word got out," Virgil says. "And nobody new has been here for quite a while."

The ghosts turn their heads in Dan's direction. They stare at him through empty eye sockets. "They can be unnerving if you're not used to them," Virgil says. "And these are the most presentable."

"What do they want?" Dan asks. He moves back toward the door.

"Some of them are hungry." Virgil points to a group at the back who hold cracked bowls and plates up over their heads.

"Feed them, then. Take what's in the cupboard and tell them to go away."

"It won't help," Virgil says. "Their throats are full of sand and they can't get anything down."

Dan feels the food from his own stomach pushing up against the back of his throat.

"In one way, they're just like you," Virgil says. "They want to find a way out of here."

"Why are they staring at me, then? You're the guide."

"Partly true," Virgil says. "I am supposed to guide *you*. It's too late for them though. And for me." He begins to fade in and out while they talk. He removes his head and holds it briefly in the crook of his arm before replacing it again.

"I thought you might have noticed," he says.

The dead move closer and closer to where Dan is standing. They hold up to him the few earthly possessions they've been allowed to save: a scrap of cloth from a child's dress. A photograph. Wreaths of dried flowers. A shaker of salt. Glass beads in a moose skin pouch.

They begin to pull at Dan's clothes with fleshless fingers. They touch his face and his hands. "Help us," they cry. "Save us!"

"Get back!" Virgil commands. The arc of his flashlight cuts through the mass of their spectral bodies. He pulls Dan back inside the cabin.

There are iron horseshoes over all the doors and windows so the dead are forced to remain outside in the growing storm, crying and praying and consoling each other in their various languages.

When lightning flashes again and again in the sky, they begin to fade away, but they leave traces of sticky filament behind on everything they've touched.

4

Dream Jumps

It's pitch dark in the house. Dan finds candles and matches in a kitchen drawer and takes them with him into the bedroom at the back of the house. He shuts the door and wedges a chair in front of it. Then he lights candle after candle and sticks each to the top of a night stand with drops of wax. He knows fire can't be trusted, but he's desperate for light.

There's a bed beside the night stand. It's neatly made and covered with a patchwork quilt. In the middle of the bed is a shoe box. Dan pushes it aside so he can sit down, then takes the lid off the box and looks inside. It's filled with snapshots, primarily of two girls. The younger one smiles a lot. Her front teeth are gone in some and back again in others. "Charlene," someone has written on the back of one of the pictures. "Grade One."

The older girl is beautiful. Innocent and exotic at the same time, like the girl next door, Dan thinks, if you lived on the Nile River. Her hair is long and blue-black. Her face the colour and shape of an almond. But the name on the back of her pictures isn't Cleopatra. It's Bee.

There are pictures of Virgil in the box as well — posing beside his boat, sometimes with the girls, sometimes with a variety of sunburned people. There's often a long string of fish between them.

And there is one picture of an older woman, grey hair cut short and business-like. She wears an apron and stands in front of a cook stove, scowling and brandishing a metal soup ladle over her head. Dan looks at her picture for a long time. He thinks he's seen her before.

There's no name written on the back of the photo so he searches the box for her face again and finds it in a snapshot at the very bottom. She's serving something from a huge bowl to a group of people seated at a plank table. Now he knows he recognizes her. And some of the other faces in the picture seem familiar. He's afraid if he goes on looking, he'll remember why.

He stuffs the pictures back into the box and replaces the lid. Then he shoves the box into a corner shelf and weighs it down with books he finds there. Even that doesn't stop him from hearing a voice calling to him from inside the box. "Useless! Useless!" He thinks it's the woman's voice he hears, although it may belong to the wind.

He crawls under the bed and covers his ears, but it's too late. Images fill his head. Sounds. Sensations. He sees himself on a dirt road. He's hurrying. Looking back over his shoulder. Then he begins to climb. He increases his pace until he's standing breathless on the edge of a cliff. He's frantic now, throwing pieces of himself away. His arms. His fingers.

Then he's back together again and he begins to run. Not too fast at first. He rests. He runs again. He feels good while he's running. He's accomplished something.

Then there's a jump in time — a dream jump, except this isn't what Dan would call a dream. There's smoke all around him now. Demons walk out of the smoke. "Get out of here," they yell. "Out of here. Out of here."

He begins to run, crashing through the underbrush. He falls. Gets up again. Pushes himself to increase his speed. Then suddenly he's moving in slow motion while everything breathes and sings around him — blades of grass. Dust. Weeds. Shafts of sunlight coming through the smoke. A raven with wings of black diamond soars above his head. "Fly," it calls to him. The trees join in and the dense voices of rocks.

Dan spreads his arms and takes off out over the valley, wheeling and turning like burnt paper in the wind.

5

I Know You

He hears furniture moving downstairs and smells food. Someone knocks on the door. "Virgil?" he calls.

"No." It's a high voice. And light. "You open the door this instant!" Something about the voice makes him feel it's safe to do that. He crawls out from under the bed and moves the chair away from the door. When he opens it a crack, he feels something whiz past him into the room.

"What are you doing here?" Charlene says. He knows it's Charlene. He's been looking at pictures of her for quite a while. She bends her elbows and rests her balled-up fists firmly on her hips. "You're supposed to come to the table. Where in the hell have you been?"

"Charlene!" The beautiful girl in the pictures comes to stand behind her. "Don't talk to him like that."

"You're Bee, aren't you?" he says.

"Yes." She raises her arms over her head and lowers them again. Every inch of progress they make leaves a line of gold in the air.

He follows the girls down the stairs and sits at the place they indicate. He's amazed at all the food on the table. There's a platter of fried ham. Another of hash browns. There are sliced tomatoes. A pitcher of orange juice. Hot cinnamon rolls. A whole sliced pineapple. Grapes. Kiwi fruit. Blueberries. Bananas. "It's morning then," he says. "I didn't think it was."

He takes the plate of food Bee offers him and begins to eat. Nothing has ever tasted this good before. He fills his mouth and chews but then can't swallow.

He puts down his silverware and looks directly at Bee. "I left myself somewhere," he says.

She gets up and comes to stand behind him. "Looks like I found you." Her voice is suddenly deeper than it was. Harsher. He feels something cold and hard poking into his neck.

"Put your hands on your head," the voice says, definitely not Bee's now. He tries to turn around but feels sharpness pressing down on his neck and does what the voice asks. "Now stand up and turn around."

"Let up, then," he says.

When the pressure on his neck eases he stands up slowly and swivels around. It's the woman from the snapshot. Same grey hair. Same frown. The only difference is she's aiming a hunting rifle at him instead of brandishing a soup ladle like she did in the picture.

"Walk backward to the sink," she says. He does what she asks again. It doesn't appear he has a choice. "Now explain to me what you're doing in my house."

"You're not Bee," he says.

She takes the question in. "Obviously. Bee's my daughter. How do you know her?" She pokes him in the shoulder with her rifle.

"I saw her picture," he says. "She's beautiful."

"You figured that out did you?" She pokes him again. "You and every other boy who gets a look at her. Tell me what you're doing here."

"Virgil brought me," he says.

"He would. And I suppose he showed you how to break in?"

"He said it would be all right." The woman's eyes are as grey as her hair. So far they seem human but he knows he'll have to be careful. "Can I ask you something?"

"Shoot," she says. She doesn't seem like the kind of person who would try to be funny.

"Are you really here? I mean, you're alive and actually in this room?"

"You'd better believe I'm here!"

"So you'd shoot me if I put my arms down? Because I don't think I'm violent and it's uncomfortable holding them over my head like this."

"Put them down then. But I warn you, I brought this gun along because the fire's got the animals all stirred up. I thought I might meet up with a bear or a mountain lion. But I can shoot you instead, if I have to."

"Okay," he says. He rubs his arms to get the circulation going.

The woman motions toward the living room. "Come over to the window so I can see your face better." She keeps a bead on him as he moves, then scrutinizes his face in the murky light coming through the window.

"I know you," she says. "You're the greenhorn who ran off from New Mountain. My God, what's happened to you? You look like hell."

"Greenhorn?" he says.

"New kid. New planter. The only thing I ever heard you called was Useless. What's your real name?"

"I lost it." He rubs his eyes, but it's just to keep her from looking at him. She may be able to read his mind.

"Sit down," the woman tells him. She points to a chair with her rifle. "You don't remember me, do you? I was the cook for your crew." He doesn't say anything. "The Green Mountain Company? Tree planters?" He still doesn't respond. "Did you get hit on the head or something?"

"This is a ghost town," he says.

"That's why I picked it. Ghosts don't bother me. Or my girls, but people can."

She gets up and looks out the window. A chipmunk runs back and forth across the deck twice before she speaks again. "Well, I can't stand around here all day talking, delighted as I am with your conversation.

"The fire's bad across the lake. They've evacuated the village. I just came by to check on my house and get a few things. Then I'm going on to my mother's in Kingman to make sure my girls are safe.

"I suppose I'll have to take you with me and leave you with the police there." She stands looking at him with her weight on one hip and the gun resting in the crook of her arm.

Dan stays in the chair while she tapes cardboard over the broken glass in the door. "I've left my truck up on the forestry road," she says. "It's a little hike from here and you look like you're about to drop, but you'll have to walk it. I'm not carrying you."

When she leaves to take a load up to the truck, she says, "Just wait here. I'll be back. I have some sandwiches in the truck I'll bring you. But leave my stuff alone."

"Okay," he says. Then as soon as she's gone he climbs up into the rocks behind the cabin and hides.

X

When the woman gets back she walks the trails close by and shouts out the only name she has for him. "Useless! Useless!" When she can't find him, she leaves.

He waits an hour or so before he ventures cautiously out from his hiding place. He thinks he may need to use it again if someone else comes, so he looks carefully at the markings on the lichen-covered rocks nearby.

"X," he says out loud. "You mark this spot." Laughter begins down in his belly. He feels it cutting its way up and out of his mouth. It makes him weep, until he laughs again. After that he loses track.

MATTI

1

KINGMAN

WHEN YOU CAME IN TO THE city from the wild fire area you were supposed to register at Kingman Regional High School, which was the main evacuation centre. We did that, otherwise Search and Rescue would think we were lost and they'd send someone out on a wild-goose chase looking for us.

Personally I didn't care if they went out or not, but then I didn't care about much.

Mrs. Stoa though, seemed to care about everything. First she didn't want to be crowded in to the high school where she wouldn't have any privacy at night. She wanted to stay with her nephew who lived in town. She was sure he'd want to take us all in. But he wasn't home when we went to his house so she left a message on his door.

Then we went back to the school and straight into the gym where someone had hung a hand painted banner with "Welcome Evacs," on it right above the Kingman Lords sign, which was professionally made and permanent. She didn't have any better luck there. There wasn't any such thing as a private section for retired English teachers.

"I feel this is inappropriate for a woman my age," she told some woman who was working her butt off setting up cots and probably could have cared less.

As for me, I didn't feel anything at all.

When we checked in at the high school Mrs. Stoa and I got a bottle of water and a gift bag with soap, shampoo, and toothpaste in it, as well as a toothbrush with the name of a local dentist printed in gold on the handle and a meal ticket for breakfasts and light suppers in the cafeteria.

We also got a pass we could use to ride the Number One bus in and out of town as much as we wanted. I'd never ridden a bus before, so I didn't realize then what a lifesaver that would be.

Marsh didn't take the gift bag. He said there was no way he could sleep inside with that many people around or even eat inside for that matter. "I've got my truck in the parking lot," he said. "I'll be there if you need me."

"Don't hold your breath," I said.

People trickled in all day from little mountain settlements like Four Mule Creek, Buckley Falls and Gumption. They were families mostly with their kids and pets and whatever else they'd had time to load up. A few old mountain men straggled in with long hair and beards.

One of them looked like the old guy who stood outside school and told me I was going to hell. He paced up and down the halls shouting about something called *The Rapture*. "Repent!" he kept saying. "The Rapture is upon us."

I thought he'd wear down but by bed time there were fifty or sixty of us trying to settle down on the cots the Red Cross had brought in and he was still going loud enough to scare little kids and make them cry.

Finally a couple of policemen led him away somewhere.

Even without him it wasn't easy to sleep. People were up and down to the bathroom all night, especially Mrs. Stoa. She made a lot of noise getting her legs over the wooden edge of her cot and more noise getting her feet down on to the floor.

People cried, and not just little kids, either. Big kids like me. Lots of adults, too. Even men. There was coughing. And whispering.

Of course I made noise myself. It was embarrassing for me, but there was no way I could get away on my own with all those people around. I put a blanket over my head until I got claustrophobic and had to take it off again.

The only ones who fell asleep right away were the snorers. That meant that the rest — the ones who might have gone to sleep if they were allowed to — didn't have a chance. Speaking for myself, I didn't get one wink.

In the morning, I was tired and wired — a T. W. to go with the T. S. I already had. I could barely breathe for all the people.

We lined up to use the bathroom and get breakfast in the cafeteria — even to take a drink from the drinking fountain, or to try and get close enough to watch what they were saying about the fire on a TV monitor in the school library.

People also lined up to read the rows of messages that were posted out in front. *Stephanie Parkinson*, as an example. *5 feet six inches tall. Blond. Blue eyes. 19 years old. Last seen at the east gate of Blackstone Wilderness. Contact Kingman Police Services. Urgent. Please phone 434-FIRE.* That was a line set up to deal with calls about people the fire had run out.

I didn't spend any time at the message board myself. There was one waiting for us from Frank when we registered saying he was safe and he'd join us as soon as he could.

I didn't expect a message from the only other person I was worried about. As far as I knew he was dead.

All I really thought about was getting away. It turned out to be easy to do that. I just walked out the door of the high school without telling anybody where I was going, flashed my bus pass at the driver and got on the Number One. I rode it back and forth most of the day so I could get accustomed to public transportation.

I picked a seat at the back of the bus and made it my new front porch swing. If anybody even looked like they wanted to sit down next to me, I glared at them and muttered things under my breath.

I'd definitely be a bus rider if I lived in a city, I think. It's relaxing and a great way to see the world.

2

THE CHEERLEADERS

IT WAS ALMOST SUPPER TIME WHEN I got back home — if you can use that word about a gymnasium. Marsh was hunkered down on the front steps and Mrs. Stoa was sitting in an aluminum fold-up chair on the lawn close by, smack in the middle of a little kids' Frisbee game. Marsh got up and walked toward me. "Matti," he said, but I held out my hand and shook my head at him.

"No!" I said.

He turned his face away like I had slapped him and kept on walking out to the street. Then he lit up a cigarette. He promised me he'd quit, so that gave me another reason to be pissed off at him.

Mrs. Stoa got up out of her chair like the metal frame was on fire when she saw me and made a bead in my direction. "Young lady!" she said. "Marshall has been driving around looking everywhere for you and worried sick. You don't know what he's going through."

"I also don't care," I said.

She actually gasped. "If your father were here," she said, "I'd suggest he ground you."

"Well, he isn't."

Mrs. Stoa stood up as tall as she could which still barely brought her up to my shoulder. "Then I'll have to do it myself."

I admit she surprised me. "You will?" I said.

"Someone has to."

What was I supposed to do after that? She was standing right in front of me. I couldn't just push her out of the way. Her bones might snap or something. Anyway I kind of admired how she didn't back down.

"You really can't do that, Mrs. Stoa," I said. "Only Frank can ground me. And as we both know, he isn't here. Excuse me, please." I stepped around her and went up the steps and into the school.

I wasn't looking forward to eating with Mrs. Stoa, but someone had apparently listened to her complaints I guess and had set up a special table in the cafeteria for senior citizens. That took care of the problem.

The high school girls who waited on that table treated her like a queen. They carried her tray for her. They even found her a little booster cushion to put in her chair.

Those girls were all dazzlingly beautiful. They wore maroon shorts and T-shirts with *Lords* written across their chests in gold. Most of them had long hair. All of them had long legs — long eyelashes and fingernails too I'll bet, if you saw them up close.

There was one girl I couldn't keep from staring at. Her hair was gold and shiny and it stood out around her head in curls like a halo. Her teeth were so white that when she smiled it made my eyes water.

"They're the school cheerleaders," someone near me said. "Aren't they wonderful?" It wasn't someone I knew so I didn't feel like I could ask what the exact purpose of a cheerleader was but I did agree they were wonderful in every way I could think of.

3

KING KOFFEE

When I got on the bus the next day, the driver said, "I'll have to charge you rent, Miss, if you don't start getting off now and then."

"Is there some kind of law about that?" I asked. How was I supposed to know he was kidding?

"No law," the driver said. "I thought you might be bored."

"Like, where would I get off and go to if I was?" I asked him. A guy behind me with a briefcase was in a toot to get on the bus but the driver stayed cool.

"You drink coffee?" he asked me.

I wasn't supposed to drink coffee so I'd actually never tried it, but I was flattered he thought I was old enough. I said, "Sure."

"Try King Koffee, then," the driver said. "I'll let you know when to get off."

King Koffee was an amazing place. There were rows and rows of coffee beans for sale in jars behind the counter with geographical names like Java and Sumatra and Tanzania. And the machine they made coffee in was so big it took two people to operate it.

At the Hot Spot, Frank just said, "Coffee, please, Allard," and Allard poured some into a cup. At King Koffee I couldn't even see the word coffee on the menu board. It was full of words that looked like they came from a foreign language. Latte. Cappuccino. Frappuccino.

"Do you like a dark or a light roast?" the guy at the counter asked me. The *barista,* he was called. A sign on the counter said, "Your barista is Chuck."

"I don't know," I said, with reference to the light or dark question.

"Okay," Chuck said. "How much bite do you like in your coffee?"

"What? Bite?"

"I'm talking about how much you want to actually feel the coffee in your mouth," Chuck said, "instead of just tasting it."

My shoulders started shaking and I felt like I was going to lose it, which I've said I hardly ever do in public. I think he noticed because he told me, "Hey. You know what I think you'll like? A caramel macchiato frappe deluxe."

"Fine," I said. I was relieved to have the ordering thing over with.

I had a story made up in case he asked to see my ID, but he didn't ask. That surprised me because according to what I'd heard at school, caffeine is addictive. It even has a half-life like certain radioactive materials. Not that I knew exactly what that meant to the workings of the body, or thought much about it.

I also didn't know how caffeine addiction compared to alcoholism. But Allard Grass had never made someone sleep off eight or ten cups of coffee on the bed in the jail at Blackstone Village before they hit the road home, so I suppose that should have told me something.

When there was a jail in Blackstone Village. When there was a Blackstone Village, at least the way I'd always known it.

At the King, they have round tables out in front with red sun umbrellas over them. I sat down at one and glanced at a newspaper someone had left behind. I was trying to look like a regular person drinking what turned out to be very sweet cold coffee, when Bee Laverdiere walked by.

She had her hair fixed in a long braid down her back. She wore shorts and sandals that had a strap going up between her big toe and the little ones. She was still beautiful, but maybe not in quite as perfect a way as the cheerleaders. Especially the golden one.

"Hi, Bee," I said. I twiddled my fingers at her and then wished I hadn't because she walked on by. I was sure she saw me. She probably just didn't want to.

At the last minute, though, she stopped and came back. "Hi," she said.

"It's Matti," I told her.

"I know." But there was relief in her voice so I think she actually didn't remember my name. "Everybody's gone from the village, I guess?"

"We had to evacuate. What about Cato City?"

"We're all down here now, but not for the same reason."

"Oh," I said. I was so lame at that kind of conversation that Bee surprised me when she sat down.

"Are you staying at the high school?" she asked me.

"Yes," I said.

"That must be exciting."

"Not really. It's crowded." A few hiccups tried to get out of my mouth after she sat down. I swallowed them.

"My little sister and I are at our grandmother's," Bee said. "There's only the one bedroom so we're crowded, too. Virgil showed up a few days ago, but we sent him to his friend's. You know my cousin, Virgil, don't you?"

"I know who he is," I said.

Bee got up and poured herself a drink of water and ice from a clear plastic pitcher on the table where the sugar and cream and stir sticks were kept. They didn't go in for real utensils at the King.

When she came back to the table Bee said, "My mom's with us now." She took little chips of ice into her mouth each time she drank and crunched on them. "She's sleeping in her tent out in back. She doesn't like being in small spaces with other people, even if it's her own family."

"I get that," I said.

"Mom was out cooking for New Mountain, but they got chased out by the fire."

"New Mountain?"

"Reforesters. Virgil worked for them when they started up last year but he didn't last long. He said he had to carry fifty or sixty pounds of tree seedlings around on his back and work twelve-hour days."

Bee's teeth made crisp little clicking sounds as she crunched more ice. "But then Virgil doesn't like working too hard or being told what to do."

She stood up a few minutes after that. "I should go," she said.

"Will you be here tomorrow?"

"Probably not. It's expensive."

"I'll buy you a coffee." I held up my bank card, which was a very uncool thing to do.

"That's okay," Bee said. She smiled. "See you sometime, though."

Marsh was parked in front of King Koffee when I came out. He had a cigarette with a long ash on it in his hand and his eyes were closed. I went out into the street and rapped really hard on the driver's side window.

Marsh's eyes flew open and he dropped the cigarette down into his crotch, which I understand is a no-no area for burns where a man is concerned. He grabbed the cigarette and stubbed it out in the ashtray, which was open and already overflowing. Then he rolled his window part way down.

"Matti! What are you doing?"

"What are you doing?" I asked him. "You and Frank both promised me you'd quit smoking after Mom died. Now look at you. Do you want to end up with lung cancer like her?"

It was a good thing he had the doors locked or I would have jumped right in, found his cigarettes and broken each and every one in half.

"I started again because I'm under stress," Marsh said. "Anyway you're not my mother. Now please get out of the street before someone side-swipes you."

I moved in tighter to his truck but otherwise didn't budge. "Can't you keep even one promise?" I asked him. Not that I had any room to talk.

Marsh turned to look at me. His eyes were red. I didn't know what I'd do if he started to cry. "I promised you I'd take you with us when the kid . . . "

"Dan," I said.

"When we took Dan to the hospital. And I would have kept that promise. He didn't run off because of anything I said. If you don't believe me . . . " He reached in his pocket for his cigarettes. Then stopped and put his hands in his lap.

"How did you find me?" I said.

"I followed the bus route, and I saw you get off here. I'm supposed to tell you that Mrs. Stoa has gone to her nephew's, right up the hill. She wanted me to move your stuff along with hers but I said not until I talk to you. If you'd talk to me."

I turned and leaned my back against the truck door. "How did Mrs. Stoa get mixed up in our lives?" I asked.

"Heaven must have sent her," Marsh said.

I turned around again to look at him and he seemed so miserable I couldn't stay mad any more. "She'll want to know everything I'm doing," I said.

"She will."

"Well, I'm not moving again as long as you're still living in the parking lot."

"I am." Marsh smiled when he said that, but it was a really weak one.

"Isn't it uncomfortable sitting up to sleep?" I asked. I knew Marsh slept in his truck a lot, but up until then I hadn't really thought about how he did it.

"What makes you think I sit up?" he asked. "I've got my sleeping bag in the back. I can roll the top back on the canopy if I want and look up at the stars. There was a meteor shower last night."

"Did you make a wish?"

Marsh shook his head. "I'm past that," he said.

4

WHAT A FIRE CAN DO

BY THE END OF THE FIFTH evacuation day, the light supper had gotten a lot lighter. Only plain chips were still available. None of the flavoured ones. There were no seconds on sandwiches. The fruit was cut into pieces and the edges of the apples especially were brown from standing a while. Still, the food was better than one of Mrs. Stoa's casseroles.

I took my sandwich and a bag of chips outside and sat on the bleachers to watch some kids playing soccer. I put the chips down next to me while I got the plastic wrap off my sandwich and right away someone sat down next to me and turned my chips into something Mrs. Stoa would love to sprinkle on top of her next tuna delight.

"Hey!" I said. I turned to look and saw a big man wearing sunglasses and a black baseball cap with Chief printed across the front.

"Surprise!" he said.

"You need to trim your eyebrows, Frank," I said back. I'd been planning on giving him the icy shoulder for saying Dan had to go to the hospital and for generally neglecting me, but that was the best I could do. When he put his arm around me for a minute and squeezed my shoulder, I even let him.

"I was looking for you this afternoon," he said. "What have you been up to?"

"Oh, the usual. Riding the bus. Spending my allowance on coffee."

"You think that's a good idea?"

"I just found out about decaf," I told him." I might be switching. Or they have lemonade."

"I'm talking about the bus," Frank said. "Be serious."

I shrugged. "No one bothers me. And you know I can handle myself."

Frank took what looked like a tiny radio out of his pocket and studied it. "It's a beeper," he said. "In case anybody needs me."

I guess they didn't because he put it back in his pocket.

"You won't be crowded in here much longer, Matti," Frank told me. "I'm trying to find a place for you."

"I have a place. It's called Blackstone Village and I want to go back there."

I suppose I would have known by then what the fire had done if I'd been listening to people talk. But I'd been tuning everybody and everything out. That's not so easy to do with Frank. He takes up a lot of room.

A fire, he told me, can eat its way through a whole forest and leave one clump of trees still standing. It can treat a town the same way.

Most of the newer buildings in Blackstone Village were burned up, including some of the big expensive summer homes I didn't like anyway. Our house was okay. And the Hot Spot.

But lots of other places weren't. The jail was gone. Our Gas and Grocery. The church. The school.

"I guess you're getting the picture," Frank said. "There isn't much to come back to, yet."

We sat for a while and were quiet. Frank had to be the first one to speak. I was just trying to hold myself together. "We should probably have a talk," he said.

"What about?" I asked, although I thought I knew the direction we were headed in. It wouldn't be an angry talk from my point of view. I was more sad than angry by then. But I thought Frank might have a few choice words for me about my behaviour.

He surprised me though. "We need to decide where you're going to school this year. And where you're going to stay while you're there."

"I thought you told me our house was okay."

"It is. But didn't you hear me say the school's gone?"

One of the kids scored a goal just then. We stopped talking and watched while he high-fived the others on his team.

"How would you feel about going to this school?" Frank asked. "They have grade nine here."

"This one?" I knocked on the bleachers with my knuckles. "Kingman Collegiate?"

Frank nodded.

"I'd just as soon you shot me." I went on about how I felt for a while and he let me. Then I changed my strategy.

"Our house is still there. And I'm sure you're going back to the village. You've probably got plans for how you're going to rebuild already."

"You know me," Frank said. "Bigger and better."

"Why couldn't I do that thing where you study at home then?"

"Distance learning?" Frank asked.

"Sure," I said. School stuff always seemed pretty far away to me anyhow. "It's a possibility. But you don't like writing and there'd be a lot of that."

"I'd handle it, though. If I had to."

"I don't know how long it will be until we get that high-speed cable in now. We won't even have electricity for a while. I suppose you could fax in your assignments when we have a generator."

Frank took off his glasses and looked at me. "You realize it's a disaster area in the village right now. It could be a discouraging place to live for a while, especially for you. Noise. Plenty of confusion."

"I'll tough it out," I said.

"If Mrs. Stoa went on staying with us, she could help you. How are you getting on with her by the way?"

"No comment," I said.

We sat a while longer. The kids were gone and the field was empty except for a few gulls looking for garbage. You didn't see ravens in Kingman like we did at home. Too much civilization, I guess.

"Anything you want to tell me?" Frank asked finally.

"Like what?" I said. I was trying to play it cool.

"Up to you."

I waited for a while to get my courage up, but in the end I just wasn't ready to talk to Frank about Dan. It still hurt too much.

Frank didn't spend the night in the gym. He said he was staying in an emergency services facility out on the edge of town, but he came in and saw where I was sleeping. "Deluxe accommodations," he said.

He also told me he'd think about my school idea. And he'd try to get back tomorrow. "Onward and upward," he said when he left. I had no idea what that expression meant.

I had a system by then that made it easier for me to fall asleep. I'd moved my sleeping bag over against the gym wall so I didn't feel so exposed and I could tic- off as much as I needed to without anyone hearing me.

I used a flashlight I'd brought in my bag to read for a while after the lights were out. Then I shined it on my hands and watched the shadows they made against the wall. After that I stared at the red exit lamp over the gym doorway until my eyes closed.

Once, just before I fell asleep, I thought I saw Dan standing underneath it. He looked exactly like I remember, except pinker, from the lamp above his head.

5

ANYBODY CAN BE VIOLENT

I WENT UP TO THE CAFETERIA to get breakfast about 8:30 the next morning. The cheerleaders were there again. This time they wore pleated skirts that were so short they barely covered their butts. I wouldn't wear anything like that myself, but it looked good on them.

The old people were gone. They'd been moved from the high school to some place more comfortable. And breakfast was just little boxes of dry cereal with fruit and milk so there wasn't a lot for the cheerleaders to do except stand behind the table where the food was set out and look stylish.

I took my cereal and went to a table by the door. I was sitting there and eating when the cheerleader with the golden hair came over to me. My heart almost stopped.

"Are you Matilda?" she asked. I shook my head because my mouth was full of cereal and I didn't want to swallow while she was looking. "You're not Matilda Iverly?"

I gave up and let the cereal go down. "Matti Iverly," I said.

"But Matilda's your real name?"

"No. My real name is Matti, like I said."

The cheerleader got a tiny little wrinkle between her perfect eyebrows. "It's only I have a message for Matilda Iverly and the description the lady gave me sounds like you."

"I suppose she was an elderly lady," I said. "And small."

"Yes. She stayed here for a while." The cheerleader unfolded the slip of paper she had in her hand. "Her name is — "

"Mrs. Stoa," I sighed.

"Then you do know her?" I was almost blinded by that smile again.

"Unfortunately," I said. "What does she want?"

"I don't know. But she's waiting downstairs by the registration table. Why don't you ask her yourself?"

"You certainly took your time," Mrs. Stoa said when she saw me. "I've been here almost an hour." She pointed to a grey-haired woman at the desk. "She wouldn't let me in," she whispered. "She said this is your home for the time being and people can't just walk in and out when they feel like it. I told her I lived here myself briefly but — "

"Good," I said. I took hold of the fluorescent sweatshirt Mrs. Stoa was wearing and pulled her through the door and outside. "How did you get here?"

"I took the bus," she said. That was hard to imagine.

"Well, I'm getting ready to go out. What do you want?"

"Your manners haven't improved, I see. But I'll ignore it because I have some news for you."

I felt like a giant talking to her. And I didn't want anyone to overhear our conversation so I hunched over and got close enough to her ear that I didn't need to yell. "I already know," I said. "Frank told me last night."

That seemed to stop her in her tracks, but only for a minute. "What do you intend to do about it?" she asked.

"I intend to go back to Blackstone Village and do my ninth grade from home."

Mrs. Stoa frowned. "I'm not following," she said.

"The fire didn't touch our house. It's still there. And Frank's going back to rebuild. I'll do my school work from home and fax it in. Or mail it." I said the last three words loudly in case the distance concept had tripped her up. Like maybe they didn't have that option for school when she was a teacher.

Mrs. Stoa gave a few fast little shakes of her head. "That isn't the news I'm talking about." She got on her tiptoes and whispered, "Dan's alive." I jerked up straight. "Yes," she said. "You heard that right."

"I'm not talking to you about this," I said. I started to walk away.

"Yes, Missy you are talking about it." Mrs. Stoa tucked her little paw into the crook of my arm and held on. "And you're talking about it with someone who knows for a fact it's true. Come with me."

"Where?" I asked her. "And how are we going to get there?"

"On the bus," she said. "And don't pretend you don't have a bus pass. I know better."

They say the world is small and it must be because Mrs. Stoa's nephew, who owned the house she was staying in, also owned King Koffee. I guess that made him the king. It also made Chuck, the barista who'd been making my coffee, the prince, because he's the king's son. Also the person Mrs. Stoa wanted me to talk to.

"Chuck," she said, "this is the young woman I told you about. Get her whatever she wants and then come and sit with us, please."

"Will it be decaf this morning?" he asked me.

"Yes, please," I said. Mrs. Stoa rolled her eyes.

We sat outside at my usual table and in a minute Chuck came out with my decaf and two glasses of lemonade. "I can only take a minute," he said. "We're getting busy."

"Tell Matti what you heard," Mrs. Stoa said.

"I don't know if it's true," Chuck said.

"Tell her anyway."

Chuck was wearing a pair of mirror sunglasses. They gave him kind of an alien look, but at the same time made it easier for me to listen to him. I could look at his face without being able to see him looking at me.

"I have a friend whose dad is a helicopter pilot," he said. "He's doing a lot of search and rescue this summer because of the fires."

Mrs. Stoa nodded her head at him while he talked like she was one of those birds you set above a glass of water to make its head move up and down.

"He and his co-pilot picked somebody up from that old ghost town across . . . " He stopped for a minute. "Across from where you used to live."

"Cato City, you mean," Mrs. Stoa said.

"He just said a ghost town."

"Probably an old mountain man," I said. "We had a few at the Evac. Centre to start with."

"No. He was young." Chuck started to get up like he was through talking, but Mrs. Stoa snagged him by the shirtsleeve.

"And what else?" she asked him.

He sat back down again. "The guy yelled at them and tried to kick my friend's dad. They were going to leave him there because he was dangerous.

Then he fell and knocked himself out so they tied him up and got him in the helicopter and flew him into town."

"What did this guy look like?" I asked.

"He was tall and he acted crazy. That's all I heard."

"Are you're sure they didn't help him fall?"

I must have looked at Chuck very hard when I asked that because he said, "Hey. Don't get mad at me. I'm just telling you what I heard."

"Matti can be very intense," Mrs. Stoa said. She looked over her glasses at me and shook her head.

"Did the guy know his name?" I asked.

"I don't think they had much of a conversation." Chuck stood up. "I have to get back to work. Customer comes first."

I was sure he'd be king himself some day if he kept that attitude. "I am a customer," I said. "And my bank balance is dropping fast because of it."

Chuck didn't sit back down, but he stayed put.

"Where did they take this guy?" I asked him.

"The police station, I guess." He looked at Mrs. Stoa. "Who's paying for the drinks?"

Mrs. Stoa looked at me.

"Now what will you do?" Mrs. Stoa asked me after I'd given Chuck my bank card and he'd gone to put the charge through.

"Try to get a loan from Frank or Marsh," I said.

"Don't avoid the question. I mean what will you do about Dan?"

"If it is Dan, which I'm positive it isn't . . . "

"Yes?"

"There's no use phoning the police station. I'd have to ask in person and then they probably wouldn't tell me anything. I'm just a kid."

"Police stations," Mrs. Stoa said. "There are two here. And I did find out something when I called the one downtown." She got little satisfied crinkles around her mouth. "If Dan was hurt, as Chuck says, or disoriented, the police wouldn't keep him.

"They'd send him to the community hospital here. But if he was violent, which means a danger to other people or even himself, they'd take him to the hospital out in Metal Springs."

"Where they take crazy people," I said.

"Mental health patients," Mrs. Stoa corrected me.

"Dan wasn't crazy." I stood up. "And anyway he's dead. So it has to be somebody else."

"I've told you your evidence for that is all circumstantial."

"And yours is all gossip, so neither one of us knows squat."

I was suddenly thirsty. I got up and poured myself a glass of ice water and gulped it down. Then I belched. That was the T. S. speaking. Manners didn't have anything to do with it.

"Even if Dan's alive," I said, "which I doubt, he couldn't be the one they found. He isn't violent."

Then I thought about how I ran Billy Butler up that tree in the sixth grade. The reason he stayed up there so long was that I was patrolling back and forth underneath with murder in my eye.

Anybody can be violent I guess, if you push the right buttons.

6

DEAD THINGS IN JARS

MRS. STOA WENT BACK TO HER nephew's to take a nap just after the meeting with Prince Chuck, and I went back to the high school. I needed to find a place where I could be alone and think about what to do. That sounded like the library, but when I got there a sign on the door said, "Closed. We're getting our collection ready for school."

I could see people in there moving furniture and pushing carts of books around so I knocked anyway. They didn't come to the door.

Next, I tried a few classrooms. Only one of them was open. I went in and saw something really disturbing in it — a huge black bookcase on the far wall with its shelves full of things in jars.

I don't mean pickles and vegetables. I mean frogs and worms and lizards and snakes. Even a baby pig with the umbilical cord still attached.

"Can I help you?" someone said. I turned and saw a woman in a white coat beside a shiny metal sink.

"Why would you kill all these things and put them in jars?" I said.

"I didn't kill them," she said. "They're from a scientific supply company."

"Then why would they kill them? And why would you want to collect them?"

The woman turned on a curved faucet at the end of the sink and filled a glass jar with water. "So we can dissect them and understand them better." The way she said it I could tell she thought I was an idiot. She drank some of the water.

"Wouldn't it be easier to understand them while they're still alive?" I asked. "I'm sure it would be easier for them."

The woman made a curve toward the door with her hand. "This part of the school isn't open to students now," she said.

"I'm not a student," I told her.

"Lucky me," she said. She drank the rest of her water.

I ended up doing my thinking outside while I walked around and around the school yard. By the time I got to the front for the third time, Marsh was there, leaning up against a cedar tree.

"Too much coffee makes you hyper," he said. "Aren't you afraid it will stunt your growth?"

"Too late," I said.

About then a family came out of the school with their suitcases. The man was one of the snorers so I should have been glad to see him go. But it actually made me a little queasy. I was just getting used to the way things were and now there were going to be more changes.

"Are you still sort of helping me out when Frank's not here," I asked him.

The sun glinted through the branches behind Marsh's head. I had to squint to look at him.

"As long as it's legal." He took the keys to his truck out of his pocket and jingled them. "Anywhere within reason you want to go?"

"There's someplace I need to go," I said. "I wouldn't say I want to go there." Then I told Marsh what I'd found out from Chuck.

"Don't get your hopes up," Marsh told me, which was the opposite of what Mrs. Stoa kept saying.

The problem was, I didn't really know what my hopes were. I wanted Dan to be the person they found in Cato City. I wanted him to be in the hospital getting better.

But if he was there, I'd have to face up to the fact that he'd pretty much run away from me. And unless the ring I was still wearing around my neck was a message, he hadn't even cared enough to say goodbye.

We tried the community hospital first. They said they couldn't give us any details because we weren't family, but they could tell us he wasn't there *then*. That sounded like he might have been there and was gone now, which was encouraging.

But it was also discouraging because if he'd been released or whatever you call it when you leave the hospital, where would he go?

We went back to the truck and sat. "I don't know what to do next," I said.

"Yes, you do," Marsh said. "If the... if Dan is in the condition you heard he was in, the hospital wouldn't just send him out into the street. Not that fast, anyway."

"So you think maybe they sent him to the mental hospital?"

Marsh started the truck. "Believe me," he said, "I'm not any more excited about going there than you are."

The road out east to Metal Springs was in horse country, all rolling hills and aspen already turning yellow for the fall. It would have been an excellent trip except for where we were going. Every time we passed a white horse I made a wish.

An appaloosa raced along beside us for quite a while. His ears were back and his tail stretched out behind him. He kept looking over at the truck like he wanted to tell us something. In a perfect world he would have been able to.

7

PERJURY

THERE USED TO BE SOMETHING CALLED a spa at Metal Springs.
Hot water bubbled out of the ground and people came there to
soak in it and get rid of their aches and pains. Sometimes they
drank the water as well.

This was all written on a sign just inside the gate to the
hospital grounds. It went on to say that fifty years or so ago,
they found out there was too much arsenic in the water so they
shut the spa down, but left the old buildings standing.

I had no idea which one of those buildings to go in to and ask
about Dan. Marsh seemed to know, though. He'd been pretty
quiet on the drive out and kind of moody, but he took me up
to the registration building like he knew exactly where he was
going.

"We're looking for a young, white male from the Blackstone
Village area," he said to the woman at the desk. "Amnesia.
Possibly in a state of agitation." He said the same thing when
we asked at the community hospital. It's amazing how you can
put everything about a person in a few sentences like that.

"Are you related to this person?" the woman asked. She
didn't look up.

"Yes," I said before Marsh could open his mouth. I wasn't going to get caught being unrelated a second time.

"You would be . . . ?"

"His cousin," I said, quick off the draw again. "Matti Iverly." I didn't look at Marsh's face when I said that. I fastened my eyes just below his chin and watched his Adam's apple move up and down when he swallowed.

"And the person you're looking for would be Iverly as well?"

"I . . . yes," I said. "But he might not know that because of his . . . "

"First name?"

"We call him Dan." That part was the absolute truth.

"Dan Iverly," the woman said under her breath. She clicked the keys on her desk top computer and moved her head up and down. Then she stopped, frowned and began moving it from side to side.

"I have no one by that name, of course, but I may have something. A young man — a John Doe, was brought here by the police. He'd been originally picked up in your general area."

She clicked and read again. "Search and Rescue were alerted by a Mrs. Laverdiere that she had found him in her house in Cato City and that he was in distress."

"That's him." I said. "That's my cousin. Cato City is just across the lake from us. And I know who Mrs. Laverdiere is."

"It also says he was uncooperative." The woman looked up at me then like she wanted an explanation.

"If somebody tied you up and flew you away in a helicopter," I said, "I imagine you'd be uncooperative too."

While she did some more checking, we waited in a little room about the size of a chicken coop. It was the opposite of fancy. The floor was bare grey linoleum. The chairs had hard, wooden seats and there were no magazines to read, although I wouldn't have been able to settle into reading anyway. I was nervous and ticcing.

The way Marsh was looking at me didn't help. It wasn't like he was angry. More like I'd hit him over the head with a board.

"Matti," he whispered. "What on earth do you think you're doing? You're not related to him."

"You have to be family to find out anything," I said. "Isn't that what they told us at the first hospital?" Marsh massaged his forehead the way I've seen him do before when he had a headache coming.

"Besides, what's a little thing like a lie when a friend's in trouble?"

"Perjury," Marsh said.

The woman from registration came back into the room then. "Dr. Charon will see you now," she announced.

8

A Danger to Himself and Others

I didn't expect Dr. Charon's office to be any fancier than the waiting room, and I wasn't disappointed. He had a huge desk, empty except for his hands on top of a file folder. A bookcase behind him overflowed with books.

That was it except for two wooden chairs like the ones in the waiting room, facing his desk. It didn't seem like you were supposed to get too comfortable or stay too long.

"I understand you think you're related to one of our John Does?" the doctor said. He was small with an oddly shaped head. I thought his voice was way too high to be coming from a man.

He didn't ask us to sit down, but we did. I figured that's what the chairs in front of his desk were for.

"Yes," I said. "His name is Dan Iverly and we'd like to take him home with us. Now, if possible."

Dr. Charon's eyes popped out a little when he heard that. "He's very ill," he said. "He's been committed."

"What does that mean?" I turned and looked at Marsh.

"It means," Marsh said and he narrowed his eyes, "that he can't leave here. And it would be breaking the law and also very unpopular if you tried to take him."

"So he's a prisoner?" I turned back toward the doctor with his unusual head. "This is a democracy. You can't just lock someone up for no good reason."

He blinked in the slow way a cat does when you've asked it a dumb question. Then he pushed back in his chair and laced his fingers across his round stomach. "How are you related to this person again?" he asked.

"He's my cousin."

"Well," the doctor said. "Your cousin attacked the men who brought him in. That makes him a danger to others."

"If it's the helicopter pilots you're talking about, I think they may have attacked him."

He went right on. "Then this same cousin assaulted a nurse while trying to fly out a third-story window shortly after he got here, making him a danger to himself, and others again. There are also signs of self-mutilation on his body. I believe that's enough reasons to keep him here for the full thirty days the law allows."

When the doctor put it like that, there wasn't a lot I could say. I was glad Marsh finally spoke up.

"Matti's just concerned about . . . " he flicked his eyes over at me and then back to the doctor. " . . . her cousin. I think she'd feel better if she could see him."

"You're her father?" the doctor asked.

"A friend of the family," Marsh said.

The doctor scooted back up to his desk and looked through the folder of papers he had there. "I don't think that's a good idea," he said. "He was close to death when they brought him in. His blood tests showed something like wood alcohol in his system. Would he have drunk that, do you know?"

"Unlikely," Marsh said.

"I don't even know what that is," I said. "Dan was just visiting us from . . . just visiting us. He went off to hike in the mountains and got lost."

"In the middle of a forest fire?"

"Before that," I said. "Anyway, there was no place to get any alcohol where he went."

"Toxins can build up," the doctor said. "The test results could have been due to lack of food and water, I suppose." He nodded like he'd experienced that first hand.

"Can we see him?" I asked again.

"I'd advise against it." The doctor closed the folder and laid his hands on top of it again. "He's heavily medicated. If you've never seen him like that before, it would be upsetting. I suggest you come back in . . . " He ran the adding machine he had inside his head " . . . a few days. They can tell you at registration which building he's in."

I couldn't believe we'd come this far and still didn't know if Dan was the guy they had here or not.

John Does, the doctor said, like the fire had flushed a lot of them out of the mountains and into the world.

I sat there, staring.

"Come on, Matti," Marsh said. "We can't do any more here today."

9

Shock Therapy

Frank came to the school again that night, just before lights out. He squatted down on the floor in the empty space where a family had been sleeping before. There were lots of spaces like that by then. And more every day.

He wasn't what you'd call limber and he had a steel plate in his back from his war injury so I knew he wasn't going to stay long in that position. He liked to be on the move, anyway. "I have to take you out of here," he said. "Home isn't an option yet. Do you have any suggestions?"

He was very business-like, so I tried to be. "Mrs. Stoa is at her nephew's house now," I said.

"I know that," Frank said.

"She invited me to stay there."

He raised his bushy eyebrows. "I thought she was driving you crazy."

"She is," I said. "Or she was, but I guess I could handle her. I have to stay in town now, anyway. I . . . something's come up."

Since Frank had quit smoking he chewed gum a lot. He liked a kind called Chewsy U that came with individual pieces wrapped in silver paper. He unwrapped a stick then and put it in his mouth. Then he rolled the paper into a tight little pellet and put it in his shirt pocket. Sometimes I found a handful of them there when I did his laundry.

"You planning on busting someone out of Metal Springs?" he asked. He didn't bring up the subject of perjury.

"I was getting ready to talk to you about that, but I guess Marsh already has." Frank nodded. "Did he tell you everything?"

"I believe he did."

I took a deep breath. "Then you know we didn't get in to see . . . the guy at Metal Springs so we don't know if it's — "

"The person you're calling Dan — "

"Or not."

"And if it is?" I didn't say anything. "He's a human being you know, Matti. It's not like taking home a lost animal."

"I know that," I said.

Frank stood up and stretched until something popped. "I don't think it's a good idea to get Marsh any further involved in this," he said. "There are things you don't know. It's hard enough for him being in town with all these people."

"But what if it really is Dan at Metal Springs and he's being tortured? What if they strap him down and shoot him full of electricity? They do that there. I heard you talking about it one time."

"It isn't considered torture. It's called electro-convulsive shock therapy. And it helps some people."

"Frying their brains?"

"There's no cooking involved," Frank said. He looked pretty stern when he said it. "But why don't you ask Marsh about it? He had it done there. He's the one you heard me talking about."

I couldn't believe what I was hearing. "Marsh had this shock therapy on his brain at Metal Springs? Why?"

Frank rubbed the spot on his back where the plate was. "He needed some help turning the war off after he got home."

"And that worked?"

"When nothing else would."

So much for my theory about Marsh's heart. The more I got out into the world, the less sense anything made. If there was a story that could clear up the confusion I felt in every direction, it wasn't in any book I knew about.

10

BILLY

MRS. STOA CAME BY THE SCHOOL in the morning and I filled her in on what had happened when Marsh and I went to the hospital. I even mentioned how nervous I was about what I'd see when I went there again. I said, "I don't think I can make it through the next two days."

"Of course you can," she told me.

We took the bus to King Koffee and walked up the hill from there to her nephew's place. It had two huge white pillars out in front with red double doors between them. Kind of like a palace, you could say.

I tried to imagine walking out that door with books under my arm and catching the bus to school. I couldn't make it happen. Mrs. Stoa wanted me to come inside and have a look around but I wasn't ready to do that yet.

Looking at it like I lived there was enough for one day.

After lunch, I watched the football team practicing out on the field behind the school. They warmed up by crashing into dummies and running up and down through rubber tires. Then the cheerleaders came out and I finally got what their main job was.

They threw each other up in the air and came down in the splits. They did somersaults and handstands. Then five girls held three other girls on their shoulders and they held one on their shoulder to make a pyramid. It was really something.

They also clapped and yelled and sang so they weren't just there for people to look at, either. Somebody should have told the guys on the football team. After the cheerleaders arrived, they gawked at them and then began crashing in to each other instead of dummies. They wore so much equipment that when they collided they sounded like bull elk locking their antlers.

It reminded me summer was almost over.

The next morning I walked around and around the inside of the school, just killing time. Finally I stopped by the railing at the top of the front stairs to tic-off and watch the tops of people's heads as they came into the building and went out again. When I turned to leave Billy Butler was coming toward me. He'd moved away when we started junior high and I hadn't seen him since.

He was smaller than I remembered. Kind of puny actually. I could have snapped him in two like a dry stick, which made me wonder why I took him seriously enough once to run him up a tree. And why even then, my tics got worse with him standing next to me.

"What is the thing you've got, Matti?" Billy said.

"Tourette's Syndrome," I said. "T. S., for short."

"I know that's what you call it. But I mean what's it like when you have it?"

I looked at him. As far as I could tell he wasn't making fun of me. "You know what it's like when you have to sneeze?"

"Sure," he said.

"And you know how you can try not to sneeze, but in the end you have to go ahead and let it happen?"

"Yes."

"That's how it is with my tics," I said. Then I changed the subject. "Are you going to school here next year?"

"I guess," Billy said. "We're burnt out. My dad's down there talking to the principal right now. Are you?"

I shook my head.

A man waved down below and yelled, "Get down here, Billy. If you can spare the time." I guess it was his father.

"See you sometime," Billy said, like we were two normal kids saying good- bye. Then he ran down the stairs.

11

There Are No Angels

Marsh and I were on the road to Metal Springs early that afternoon. The receptionist said we could find Dan in Building 3B. She also told us how to get there. "Show the guard at the door this slip of paper," she said, "and he'll let you in."

I took the paper and we started walking. The closer we got to Building 3B, though, the slower Marsh walked. Finally he stopped completely.

"Come on," I said. "Let's get this over with."

"I can't, Matti," he said. His face was grey and he had beads of perspiration all over his forehead. "It's a secure building. They'll lock us in on whatever ward Dan's in. I'm sorry, but I just can't go in there."

I didn't ask Marsh how he knew so much about the hospital. After what Frank told me, I could pretty much figure that out.

"I'll go in by myself," I told him. "There's a guard there. What could happen?"

Marsh tried to convince me to go back to town and wait until Frank could come with me but I dug in my heels.

I was done with waiting.

The door to 3B was heavy, without any glass in it. Marsh stood beside me while I rang the bell and waited for the guard to come. "I'll be waiting for you right here," he said.

In a minute we heard a click. Then a voice came through the door asking what we wanted.

"I want to see Dan Iverly," I said. "I'm his cousin."

"Iverly?" I heard paper shuffling. After what seemed like forever the voice asked, "He that John Doe?"

"No," I said. "He's . . . " but the door opened then and I went inside.

"Ward C," the guard said. "Up the stairs. Ring the bell again."

I went up where he pointed and then stopped at another locked door. I was reaching out to ring the bell when someone on the other side of the door began to howl.

There was something wild and lonely about the sound, like the call a mountain lion made when he hung around our place a few summers ago.

I thought it was Dan.

And I thought I was too late, they'd already done something to him. I wanted to scream myself and then run away. But I didn't. I pushed the bell and waited.

The howls started again just before someone came to the door. He was big, like a mountain that moved on white rubber-soled shoes.

"I want to see Dan Iverly," I said. My voice was higher than I wanted it to be.

"I know," the nurse said. "The guard phoned up."

When I went through the doorway I saw an old lady in her nightgown standing in the hall. She opened her mouth to scream again. "Enough now, Betty," the nurse said. "This visitor is not for you."

The woman turned and walked down the hall.

"I'll bring Iverly out to you." The nurse unlocked the door to what he called the coffee room and let me inside. "He's walking today, but I can tell you he was flying when he came in."

I would have had some coffee while I waited, except there wasn't any in the coffee room. There wasn't any tea, either. Also no cups, plastic or paper. Not even a drinking fountain. Just two tables and altogether, five chairs with the legs wrapped in plastic foam.

I sat down at one of the tables. Two men were sitting at the other and arguing. Then the one that was older started to cry.

I didn't have the greatest feeling about being locked in with them.

The doctor said it would be upsetting to see Dan when we were here before. That he would look better if I waited a few days. But if how he looked was *better*, I couldn't even imagine what *worse* would have been.

The guy that shuffled in to the coffee room a few minutes later just stood in the doorway. His eyes were only halfway open. He held his head off to one side. I wouldn't even have known he was Dan, if the nurse hadn't led him over to a chair at the table where I was sitting.

"This is your cousin," he said to Dan.

Dan slowly swivelled his head around to look at me.

All I really needed him to do was say my name. That would have been enough.

Instead he said, "You tricked me." And then he added, "You're not Bee."

He might as well have punched me in the stomach. "No," I said. "I'm Matti. Remember? I'm your angel." I'm embarrassed to admit it, but it's what I said.

"There are no angels," he told me.

Then he put his head down on the table and let his eyes close all the way down.

12

ANOTHER WEIRDO

MARSH WAS WAITING JUST WHERE I'D left him. He wasn't the colour of old newspaper any more, which was good because I probably was. "What's wrong?" he said. He came over and stood beside me. "Wasn't it Dan?"

"Yes," I said. "It was." I started walking toward the parking lot. "I'm not coming back here again. And don't ask me why."

"Wait up, Matti!" Marsh said. "That building over there's the cafeteria. Let's get something to drink."

I didn't feel like doing that. I needed to get someplace dark and private where I could let myself go. My legs wouldn't hold me up though. I sat down on a bench and waited while Marsh went into the cafeteria.

While I was sitting there alone, a guy walked by wearing baggy jeans held up with rainbow suspenders. His hair came to a point in the middle of his head, and not because he combed it that way. Not combing it at all was more like the problem.

In some ways he could have been Dan's age. In others he was younger and older at the same time. "The sky's falling," he said. I hoped he'd keep on walking if I didn't pay any attention to him, but he stopped and came back. "I wouldn't sit here if I were you."

"Another weirdo," is what I thought. Then it dawned on me that people probably thought the same thing about me at times and I was ashamed.

"I'm waiting for someone in the cafeteria," I told him. "I can't leave."

"No one takes Howard seriously," he said.

"Howard?" I asked. I looked both ways but there wasn't anyone near us. "Is he . . . like someone you know?"

"You should move," he said again, but he smiled. It made him look a lot younger — almost like he was a little kid.

Marsh came out of the cafeteria about then. I stood up and started toward him. "Good bye," I said to the suspenders guy.

"Good bye," he said. "Be careful."

"Who was that?" Marsh asked when we met in the middle of the green space.

"Somebody different." I took the can of coke Marsh handed me. I drank it very fast and then belched two or three times. I only felt a little relieved.

Marsh and I walked slowly back to the parking lot. "I was in 3A once," he said. "I thought I could go back in that building again but . . . "

"Frank told me about the electric shocks you had. Did they help you?"

"I'm still here," he said.

When we got to the truck, I finally told him that Dan didn't recognize me. I left out his comment about Bee. I could drink ten cans of pop and belch a hundred times and that would still stick inside me.

"He's medicated," Marsh said. "He could probably look at his own hand and not know what it was."

"He said there are no angels. Then he put his head down on the table like I wasn't there."

"Matti, it's just rambling. These drugs they put you on to straighten you out can be brutal. You don't want to give up yet."

"You told me not to get my hopes up."

"Well," Marsh said, "maybe I was wrong."

I did want to give up, though. Bee had been out to the hospital to visit Dan. Her mother must have checked with Search and Rescue and then with the police and found out where they'd taken him. They'd talk to her since she's the one who had Dan picked up. Then she went to visit him and took Bee with her.

It didn't really make any difference how Bee got there, though. Dan had met her and now I was toast. He couldn't even remember my name.

I suppose he was bound to meet a beautiful girl eventually. They were everywhere. Now that I'd seen the cheerleaders, I knew that.

I also knew I would never be one of them.

13

THE PALACE

I MOVED IN WITH MRS. STOA the day after the visit to Metal Springs. I think it was a Monday. The house was large enough for three or four families to live in full time and not bump into each other. The kitchen was especially amazing.

The appliances were all silver coloured and the counter tops had silver flecks in them. And instead of a normal table and chairs, there was something called an island in the middle of the room with high metal stools around it.

The odd thing about having a kitchen like that is there was never anybody home to cook in it — except for Mrs. Stoa, of course, and she's no gourmet. The King was off travelling with his girlfriend the whole time I was there. And the Prince was always at work.

I didn't mind all the space, though. I had a big room upstairs. I was in it moping when Frank came to see me just after I'd moved in. He knocked on the door.

"Not bad," he said when he came in.

"I guess not."

"A little small, maybe." After that hilarious joke he got serious. "We won't have the power back on in the village for several weeks yet, so Mrs. Stoa has you registered for the distance program. You can start tomorrow, if you want."

"Maybe day after tomorrow," I said. "I'm pretty tired."

"Meeting your cousin wear you out?" Frank asked.

"Maybe you should have me put in jail for impersonating a relative."

"It wouldn't be any use, Matti. You'd just find a way to break out again."

That was true.

"What I want you to do," Frank told me, "is start the distance work so we can see how it goes. Stay out of Mrs. Stoa's hair and . . . what day is this?"

"Monday," I said.

"On the weekend, you and I and Marsh are all going out to the hospital to sort things out there."

"Whatever," I said. And then I asked, trying to sound casual, "Where is Marsh, anyway? Is he still staying in the high school parking lot?"

"He's back in the village. There's a lot of work for him to do there, but he'll drive back down. Are you changing the subject?"

I was trying to. "I can't go out to Metal Springs," I said.

"I thought you promised to save your cousin's life."

"That was quite a while ago," I said, "before I found out certain things." I started to cry a little.

"There's no expiry date on promises.," Frank said.

That got me going. "He doesn't remember me, Frank," I wailed. "I'm not beautiful enough. And . . . and you know he isn't really my cousin."

I was actually bawling by then. My nose ran. Big, fat tears rolled down my cheeks and plopped onto my shoulders.

Frank put his arm around me like before, only tighter. It felt good and fatherly. I leaned into his chest for just a minute.

As soon as he left, Mrs. Stoa came to the door. "Let me in, please, Matilda," she said. When I didn't, she barged right on in. Technically it was more her room than mine, but I still didn't appreciate it.

She perched on the end of the bed. "I heard what you said to your father about Dan," she said.

"Don't you know it's not polite to eavesdrop?" I rolled over and turned my back to her.

"I don't give a fig about politeness at this time in my life. It's the truth I'm after," Mrs. Stoa said, like she was Batman, the Caped Crusader.

I didn't have any fight left in me by then, so I didn't answer her back.

"What is it?" she said. "I thought you'd be happy to know Dan's alive."

I rolled over and looked at her. "But he's in love with Bee Laverdiere. I knew if he saw her that would happen. It's Romeo and Juliet all over again."

"Oh, dear Lord," Mrs. Stoa said. "You have to pick the stories you let into your life, Matilda. That particular one is such a trap for a young girl. Killing herself because she can't have a boy she's only known a few weeks."

"I saved his life!" I said. "I wanted to be important to him."

"Fate saved his life," Mrs. Stoa told me. "But you were important. You were there to greet him when he came out of the fire, just like your namesake greeted Dante."

I rolled over fast and sat straight up. "Mrs. Stoa," I said. "I've told you over and over, I am not Matilda.

"And why would I want to be a greeter, anyway? I've seen what they do at discount stores in Kingman. They meet you when you come in and ask if you want a shopping cart. There's no status in that."

I let out a lot of air and lay down flat on my back with my arms folded over my chest like a body in a funeral parlour.

14

Beauty

I was willing to start distance learning right away, but it turned out I still needed books to do it. Mrs. Stoa and I spent quite a while trying to figure out how to order them on-line. We finally accomplished that but then neither one of us had a credit card to pay for the order. That was half a day wasted.

I decided to take a ride on the Number One to recover. I got on opposite King Koffee and rode to the end of the line. After the bus turned around and headed back toward town, it stopped at the high school and a crowd of kids got on. In the middle of them was the golden cheerleader. She looked almost as amazing in normal clothes as she did in her uniform.

She took the seat in front of mine. I watched while she dug in her purse and got out a mirror. Then she held it up and studied her face in it, section by section.

First she examined her left eye. She got out a little pencil and made a black line on her eyelid. Then she wet her finger with her tongue and smudged most of the line out.

She did the same thing to her other eye. After that she wiped off her lipstick and put it on again.

She took out her cellphone and held it over her head toward me. I didn't know what she was doing. Did she want me to say something into it? There was a tiny click. Then she brought the phone around again and looked at it.

It eventually dawned on me that she had a camera in her phone. She'd taken a picture of the back of her hair to see how it looked. I guess she was pleased. She put the phone away but she went on checking out her reflection in the bus window.

Up until then, I'd thought beauty was something you were born with. It had never occurred to me before how much work it took.

15

A Balloon without Air

Since I'd had a frustrating day I went in to King Koffee to recover. I'd just finished giving my order when someone in line behind me said, "Matti?" I turned around.

"Hi," Bee said.

I stood there trying desperately to think of an excuse to run out the door when Chuck called out loud enough for everyone to hear, "Cherry lemonade for Matti."

"Why don't you come and sit outside," Bee said. "My cousin Virgil's out there, too."

I hadn't seen Virgil when I came into the shop but it was definitely him at the table. I sat across from him, and Bee scooted her chair up next to his. I could tell from the way the tree branches near us swayed that the wind was blowing slightly, although I didn't feel the air moving on my skin. It was always that way with the weather in Kingman. It wasn't quite real.

"It's Marty, right?" Virgil said.

"Matti," I told him.

"I wasn't sure you'd stayed in town," Bee said. "I haven't seen you around school much."

"I'm not in school the way you are," I told her. I explained about distance learning, or what I knew about it. I slurped my lemonade fast, hoping to get away.

"You're not missing much," Bee said. "Kingman Collegiate is very big."

She and Virgil both had cups of coffee. She sipped at hers. He stirred spoonful after spoonful of sugar into his.

"I'm taking Bee shopping," he said. "Her mom won't leave the backyard and she's hidden the keys to the truck so I bought an old beater."

"Mom's mad at Virgil," Bee said.

"Picks up her gun if I try to come near her." Virgil stirred in his fourth spoonful of sugar.

"Exactly how I feel about you, Bee," I thought. In my lap and under the table my hands strangled her.

"What did you do?" I asked Virgil.

"Nothing. But my aunt thinks I helped some kid break into her cabin. She recognized him because he worked for New Mountain when she was there."

"Those tree planters?" I asked.

Virgil nodded. Then he stopped stirring and looked at me. "Actually, it was your friend who broke in."

"My friend?"

"Right. The guy with amnesia."

The lemonade from the bottom of my glass had a sour streak in it. It caught in my throat and I almost choked. "What are you talking about?"

Bee got up and brought me some water. I took a few loud gulps from the glass. "Remember I said my mom was cooking for New Mountain? She recognized the guy who broke in because he worked there too. The only name she knows for him is Useless. I guess he was, where planting trees is concerned."

I sat there goggling at Bee.

"Anyway," she said. "He took off one night. I don't know when that was. Then Mom found him in our cabin when she stopped by to pick up some things."

"But," I said, "I don't understand how he got over to Cato City."

Virgil finally stopped stirring and looked at me. "I took him in my boat," he said.

"And then went off and left him again?"

"Whoa!" Virgil tipped back in his chair. "Now you're mad at me, too."

"Of course I'm mad," I said. "When did this happen? When did you take him across?"

Virgil closed his eyes and thought for a minute. "Early in the morning, I guess." He thought some more. "You guys were evacuated that evening."

I glared at him. "Why would you do a thing like that?"

Virgil shrugged and sat forward again like he was cool with what he'd done, but I saw a little fire in his eyes. "It's still a free country," he said, "and he wanted to go."

This time I got up to get my own water. When I sat down again I said, "And then you took him to Bee's house so he'd be safe?"

Virgil looked from Bee to me and back again. "No," he said. "I didn't exactly take him to the cabin. I . . . " His coffee must have been cold by then but he stirred, anyway. "Okay, I screwed up. I was tired because I'd been up all night . . . checking some houses in the village I'd been looking after." He glanced at Bee out of the corner of his eye. "I thought I'd go back to my place and pick up some things, get a few hours of sleep and then come down here."

"And you left him there," I said.

"He wasn't around when I was ready to go."

"Do you know that if Mrs. Laverdiere hadn't called the Search and Rescue about him, he'd be dead now? That's what the doctor at the Metal Springs hospital told me."

"He's in Mental Springs?" Virgil said.

I thought that was crude. "You already know that's where he is," I snapped. I stood up and pointed at Bee. "Or at least she does. She's been out to see him."

Bee's jaw fell open. "What?"

"Well, haven't you?" I said.

"Matti, I don't have any idea what you're talking about. I've never even met this guy."

Bee wasn't glamorous compared to one of the Kingman cheerleaders. Her hair was a little messier than theirs. And one of her front teeth overlapped the other, but there was something about her. When I looked at her I knew she was telling the truth. It just came shining out.

"Well," I said. I sat down. "I don't know what to say, then."

"I told him I'd give him a ride to Kingman in my boat," Virgil told me. "But he wasn't there when I got back from my place. I thought he'd gone."

"Just flew away?"

"I'm sorry," he said again. "I already said I screwed up."

"We'll take you out to see your friend if you want us to," Bee told me.

"Maybe sometime," I said. "Frank and Marsh are taking me out tomorrow."

I felt like a balloon with all the air gone out of it. I was embarrassed about the meltdown. Also shocked, and other things I couldn't name so the conversation kind of petered out.

Virgil and Bee left, but I stayed on, trying to make sense out of what I'd heard. I believed Bee when she said she hadn't been out to see Dan. But if they'd never met, how did he know her name?

I sat at the table so long, Prince Chuck came out to see if I was all right. Or maybe he just wanted to sell me more lemonade. He did take his work very seriously.

I'd watched Virgil and Bee as they walked away down the street. When they'd gone a little ways, he took hold of her hand. They kept walking together like that for as long as I watched.

That didn't make sense to me, either.

16

CHICKEN LEGS

MRS. STOA WAS UP ON A step stool in the palace kitchen when
I got back, reaching out as far as she could for something. It
brought her skirt up and focused my attention on her legs. I've
seen chicken drumsticks that were fatter. It's a wonder they
could hold her up.

"What are you looking for?" I asked her.

"A jellyroll pan," she said. "I thought I'd make us a jellyroll."
She rattled around for a while. Then she climbed down empty
handed.

No jellyroll I guess. Whatever that is.

I told her about meeting Bee and Virgil and about what they
said.

Then I made the mistake of telling her how Bee and Virgil
were holding hands after they left.

"What do you think that means?" she asked me.

"It means they might be . . . you know. But they're cousins!"

Mrs. Stoa clucked her tongue. "A little hand-holding doesn't
mean anything, Matilda. You have a lot to learn about affection."

This from an old woman who walked around on chicken
legs.

17

How It Went Down

FRANK DROVE US OUT TO THE hospital. Marsh rode in the front with him, and I sat in the back. I didn't talk to begin with. Just turned my head and looked out the window. I wasn't sure what to wish for anymore so I didn't pay attention to the white horses we passed, but I did notice that same appaloosa running along beside us for quite a ways.

Every time I took my eyes away from it, I saw Frank watching me in the rear view mirror. Eventually, I leaned forward so I could stick my head in between the two bucket seats at the front. "I suppose you want me to talk to that doctor again and confess that I made up Dan's name."

"Not necessary," Frank said.

"So he's not . . . ?"

"Pressing charges?" Marsh seemed very relaxed riding up in front with Frank. If he'd been a dog he would have had his head out the window with his ears streaming behind him in the wind.

Frank pulled over to the side of the road and stopped. He swivelled around to look at me. Marsh stayed facing the dashboard, but now he watched me in the mirror. "This is how it went down," Frank said. He loved to sound like he was in the know.

"I eventually got the doctor on the phone. I told him I was working with emergency social services in Kingman, checking up on people missing from the Blackstone Village area after the fire."

"That's all true," I said.

"I gave the doctor Marsh's description of the kid."

"Dan," I said.

"The doctor told me they had someone matching that description there. Then he told me about the infamous visit by Matti Iverly, who claimed to be his cousin and claimed the kid's name was Dan Iverly. And I said I knew who you were."

"You said you were my father?"

"I said we were related and that you were usually reliable." He waggled his eyebrows.

"What did he say then?"

"He said thanks. It sounded to me like he was happy to have one less John Doe on his books. He called me back later and told me the patient in question had regained some of his memory and affirmed that his name was in fact Dan Iverly." Frank snapped his fingers. "Just like that."

We drove again for a while and then I remembered I hadn't told Frank what I'd learned from Bee and Virgil. I filled him in. "Mrs. Laverdiere didn't remember exactly when Dan quit planting," I said, "but he must have been alone out in the wilderness for quite a while."

"I've got someone checking into missing person accounts," Frank said. "No one of the kid's description has been reported missing around here."

He glanced at Marsh. "It would help of course to have fingerprints."

"Dan wandered in to Mrs. Laverdiere's house in Cato City after he left the village," I said. "She found him there and tried to take him to Kingman, but he wouldn't go. She's the one who sent Search and Rescue out to find him."

"Want me to go and talk to the Laverdiere woman?" Marsh asked Frank. "Ask her his name?"

"She doesn't know it," I said. "I don't think she'll talk to you, anyway. She threatened to shoot Virgil."

"Lots of people have threatened to shoot Virgil," Frank said, "mostly fathers. But if she has a gun in the city, maybe we'll just notify the police."

"Wait a minute," I said. "I told you this because I thought it would help Dan. Not so you could go around acting like you're in charge again. Is that what you intend to do when we get to the hospital?"

"Instead of what?" Frank asked.

"Instead of . . . just . . . going along and acting normal."

"You know me, Matti," Frank said. "You know me."

18

The Chains Are Off

I started toward building 3B, but Frank stopped me. "This way, Matti," he called. "The doctor told me he's been moved." We walked along the gravel path to a different building with 5A on the front. The door was open on this one and there were no grids on the windows.

Frank gave Dan's name to someone at the desk. She pointed us to his room but he wasn't in it.

"He's in the green space," another big nurse said. He wasn't wearing white. He had on dark blue pants and a long, loose top with chilli peppers printed all over it.

"I thought you had him locked up," I said.

"We took the chains off several days ago," the nurse told me. Everyone smiled except me.

Frank and Marsh and I went out the back door of the building. The green space turned out to be brown, although you could see it had been green before the grass gave up in the drought. There were a lot of trees. We crunched over their dead leaves when we walked.

People strolled by, sometimes alone, sometimes in pairs or small groups. A family with two little kids was having a picnic over by a chain-link fence. Two old men played chess, holding the board between them on their knees. Nobody seemed to be suffering.

We walked all around and didn't find Dan. We were just going to the cafeteria to check if he might be there when I saw the guy with the rainbow suspenders sitting on the grass by an old brick building.

I considered walking over and asking him what condition the sky was in that day, but he was talking to someone and I didn't think I should interrupt.

The suspenders guy seemed to remember me, though. He stood up, took a few steps in our direction and then stopped. Frank and Marsh came and stood beside me. "That him, Matti?" Frank asked.

"Not the guy with the suspenders," I said.

"Weren't you talking to him when we were here before?" Marsh asked.

"Just about the weather."

The suspenders guy started walking toward us again. That's when the person he was with stood up and came in our direction as well.

It was like adjusting binoculars when you're out looking for birds. Focus. Refocus. Gradually that second person became Dan. Not the one I saw in 3B.

The one I knew. Or thought I knew.

He'd changed again. He stood much straighter now. His hair was a colour somewhere between green and black. But he was wearing the Blackstone Village Volunteer Fire Department shirt I'd given him.

Frank walked right up and held out his hand. "Dan Iverly?" He said it like he had stepped out of a western movie where he was the sheriff and was making an arrest, but Dan looked more confused than scared.

"What?" he said.

"You're Dan Iverly?" Frank said it slower the second time.

"He is," the suspenders guy said. He held his hand out to Frank and Frank shook it, but he kept looking at Dan.

"There's no record of a missing person matching your description anywhere in the system," Frank told Dan.

"Oh?" Dan said. "Sorry."

Frank eyeballed him.

"Well," he said, "an inconvenient detail." He shook hands with Dan after that, but I could see he was still on red alert. "I'm Frank Iverly, which seems to make me your uncle."

Marsh had moved to stand on Frank's right. Frank introduced him. "This is Marsh, who took care of you when you were in Blackstone Village living in my office, as I'm told. I'm the mayor up there by the way. And the voluntary fire chief, Justice of the Peace and just about anything else I need to be."

He forgot to mention dogcatcher.

"You remember Marsh, of course," Frank said.

Dan looked like he'd been under two feet of water and needed to come up for air. Still, he managed to nod his head.

I tried to stay behind Frank but he tugged my arm and got me out in front of him. "And this," he said, "as I'm sure you'll remember, is your cousin Matti."

No reaction from Dan. It was like the cartoon about what dogs hear when we talk to them. "Blah, blah, blah, blah, blah, Matti." Like that.

I took the chain with the ring on it from around my neck and put it in his hand. After that he gave me a watery smile.

We went to the cafeteria for a drink, which gave everybody something to do with their hands and an excuse for not saying much. Dan apologized for squinting. He said he was having trouble with his eyes because of the medication and he couldn't see us very well. After that he kept his head down and didn't talk.

One thing happened that made me hopeful. As we were leaving, Dan said, "Matti?" He held the ring up. I noticed his hands were trembling almost like mine do sometimes.

"Thank you," he said.

I know it wasn't much, but I had the feeling he would have said more if Frank hadn't been watching him like a hawk.

We said goodbye to Dan. Then as Frank and I were going to the parking lot, the suspenders guy, who I'd decided must be called Howard, caught up with us and asked for a ride into the town of Metal Springs. He said he lived there.

"You're not a patient here?" Frank asked him. He'd want to know that of course. It wouldn't do for the mayor of Blackstone Village to assist anyone in breaking out of a mental hospital.

Howard shook his head. "I'm a volunteer."

We had to wait a bit for Marsh. He went back because he said he'd left something in the cafeteria. I had a bad feeling I knew what it was.

Metal Springs, the town, was even smaller than Blackstone Village, and not doing as well, even considering our fire. There was just a rundown gas station and convenience store — nowhere near as nice as the Gas and Grocery had been, and — some boarded-up houses that were probably okay a hundred years ago.

"Where do you live?" Frank asked Howard.

"You can just let Howard off anywhere here," Howard said.

We stopped at the gas station and he got out. "Thank you," he said. Then he very seriously directed us out to the road like we were in heavy traffic instead of the only vehicle in sight.

"You think he's squatting in one of those old buildings?" Marsh asked Frank when we were driving again.

"What do you mean, squatting?" I said.

"Living," Marsh said.

"Illegally," Frank added. "But relax, Matti. I'm not going to investigate. I have other fish to fry."

19

ONE RIGHT THING

I FELT MORE AND MORE SURE that Dan had wanted to tell me something when we were there, but I'd practically been forbidden to go out to the hospital alone. After about a week of not knowing, I couldn't stand it anymore.

I told Mrs. Stoa I needed a break from the schoolwork she was torturing me with, and in the afternoon I rode the Number One down to the main terminal. I found out there how to transfer to a bus that ran directly out to the hospital.

While I was waiting for it, I saw Howard coming out of a shop across the street carrying a big bouquet of flowers. He crossed toward me when I called out to him.

His hair was combed down flat on his head except for a clump in the back that wouldn't cooperate, and he was wearing a striped necktie. "You're all dressed up," I said. "Where are you going?"

"To visit the family," he said.

Now that he was closer I noticed he was carrying three separate bouquets. Each one was wrapped in its own cellophane package. "Does your family live in town," I asked.

"Rolling Acres," Howard said. He fiddled with a teddy bear attached to one of the bouquets.

If I had lived in Kingman I would have known what Rolling Acres was and I would have left it at that. I didn't live in Kingman, though. And I've already mentioned that I go straight ahead better than I back up. "Where's that?" I asked.

"Out south of town." Howard's bus pulled up then. "It's good you found Dan," he told me as he was boarding. "Family's the best thing. You can never have enough."

I watched as his bus pulled away. "Rolling Acres Cemetery," the sign across the back of the bus read.

I gave myself a little pinch on the arm.

Dan was sitting in front of the Registration Building when I got to the hospital, almost like he was expecting me. Right away I plunged in with questions again. How did he meet Bee Laverdiere was the first one.

He said he didn't know. He gave that answer to all my questions, except for a couple of times when he said, "I don't remember."

I did one thing right, though. I gave him the fudge I'd brought with me. He put a piece in his mouth and a strange look came across his face.

"Millionaire Fudge," he said, like it was the name of a beautiful poem. He closed his eyes and chewed. Then he opened them and said, "This I remember. You gave me some before."

"Yes," I said.

"And you have a sister." He stopped chewing. "Are you the beautiful girl who fed me?"

"Yes," I said. "I am." I didn't even feel embarrassed.

I was the one who was flying when I left the hospital. Dan was starting to remember things! Maybe he had true things and dream things mixed up, but I could overlook that.

He remembered me!

I had to hold on to the bus stop sign to keep from floating away.

20

IN THE SYSTEM

IT WAS SEVEN IN THE EVENING and the you-know-what was hitting the fan when I got back to the palace. Buses don't run from the hospital to Kingman as often as I'd thought.

Mrs. Stoa had managed to get hold of Frank on his pager and tell him I was missing. He roared up just after I got there and took the front steps two at a time. I thought for a minute he was going to hug me when he saw I was home. Then he got control of himself.

"Where have you been?" he demanded.

"Calm down, Frank," I said. "I just went out to see Dan and I had transportation complications."

"You went out there alone?" He actually had a squeak in his voice.

"On the bus," I said. "And I wasn't alone. There were quite a few people from the hospital on it when I came back. Big nurses, I mean. Not just patients."

"You . . . " Frank shook his head. "I want you to promise me you won't do that again."

"I can't," I said. "I have to go back. Dan's remembering things now. He remembers me."

Frank frowned and looked down at his feet, which was strange behaviour for him. Then he said, "My contact got a positive on him, Matti." That put an end to the joyfulness of the day.

"What're you talking about?" I said. Frank didn't answer. "Marsh took Dan's glass from the cafeteria, didn't he? You got his fingerprints. You just couldn't resist."

Frank fluttered his eyelashes like he had grit in his eyes. "He's in the system," he said.

"Who cares?" I snapped. "What'd he do, anyway? Steal food because he was starving?"

"He hasn't broken any laws I know of," Frank said. "That's not why he's in the system."

'Well, why then?"

Frank measured out his words very carefully. "Because twelve years ago, when he was eight, his parents had him fingerprinted as part of a Missing Child Program."

"He was kidnapped, you mean?"

"No. They had it done to make it easier to find him if he was. Or if he got lost."

"And did he?"

"The only other thing I know is, he and his family were involved in a car accident a year later. Everyone was killed except for him."

I sat down on the steps and stared at Frank. I wasn't sure if I felt better or worse, knowing Dan was an orphan.

"Do you want to know his name?" he asked.

The answer to that was easy. "Not until he does. As far as I'm concerned he's my cousin Dan Iverly until he tells me he doesn't want to be."

DAN

1

Ghosts

THE ROOM IS FULL OF GHOSTS and demons. It's smoky, but I can see well enough to tell that. They open and close their mouths like fish pulled out of water. Only one of them can speak. "Who are you?" it says. "Tell us your name." This is followed by two sharp blasts on a trumpet.

A raven beats its wings at the window as a warning but I'm already vigilant. "I don't have a name," I say. I repeat the words over and over until they let me go.

2

WALKING

I'M IN A DIFFERENT ROOM NOW. It sounds and smells like lemons. "Time to get moving," a voice says. It's a man's voice. Not unkind. Definitely not a ghost's.

There's a body with the voice. And a head with an aura around it. I feel as light as a sheet of paper. I'm afraid I may blow away.

"I think I'll stay in bed," I say.

"I think you won't." The body that belongs to the voice makes me sit up and slide my legs over the edge of the bed. It picks me up, folds me like a letter and pockets me. We walk around.

3

THE H PILL

I'M SITTING IN A CHAIR IN the lemon room. A person who says he's my nurse is shaving me. He tips my head back and presses the razor blade against my throat. I'm so weak I let him.

This nurse tells me it isn't ghosts I've seen. Or demons. They're hallucinations. I'm in a hospital and what I have seen are doctors. They're the ones with the questions.

There's no smoke in the air here, either. The reason I can't see very well is because of a pill they're giving me. The name of it begins with H. He hands me one now. Pronounces it for me.

I have to swallow the H pill. If I don't, the doctors will shoot it into my veins. "It's not forever," the nurse says. "You'll get your eyes back again." I wonder what else the doctors have of mine. My hand is shaking when I reach it out.

4

GRAVITY

IT'S JUST THE ONE DOCTOR I talk to now. He always sneezes when I come into the room. "So," he says. "Do you know your name today?" He starts out like this every time. I tell him I'm not sure I have one.

"You're not sure?" he says. "Last time you were sure you didn't have one. Why's that?" He's holding something in his hand — a pencil or pen. It begs to write.

"If I'm human, I have a name. But am I human?"

"What do you think?" He sneezes again into the crook of his elbow.

"I think," I say, "that . . . " I scratch my nose. "I'm not sure." The pencil drops down and writes something.

Now he changes the subject. "How are you feeling?" It's rhetorical. "Still seeing things?"

"I see you," I say. I don't mention the headless guy standing behind him with a flashlight. According to the nurse, the headless guy isn't really there.

Another subject change. The doctor likes to try and confuse me. "How did you get out of the fire area?"

"I've already told you," I say. He doesn't like the way I answer this question, but I can't help that. My answer is all I have now.

"Tell me again."

"I flew."

"In a helicopter?"

He knows I don't mean that. "On my own. I could fly then. I've told you that."

He gives me several reasons why that isn't possible. Gravity is one of them. I tell him I was chased by demons who wanted to capture me and possibly suck out my soul. He says that's also impossible.

"The dead are always with us," I say. He doesn't buy that either.

He turns a desk lamp on and shines it on something there. Unless it's the headless guy's flashlight I see. Unless he's the one who wants to know if I remember.

"Do you recall breaking into a cabin somewhere out on Blackstone Lake?" the doctor asks.

"No," I say. "I don't."

"But you understand you did that? That actually happened?"

I don't understand that. I don't remember it. "I remember flying," I say. More writing. Another sneeze.

"What about hearing things?"

"I hear everything."

"Including voices?"

"I hear voices. Of course."

"Oh?" Up comes the pen. Or pencil.

"I just heard one. Didn't you ask me a question?"

The pencil comes down again and writes something. Smart ass, probably. However a doctor would say that professionally.

He blows his nose into a white square — two blasts in a low register. I have the impression he's brought an instrument into the room. A tuba, possibly. Or a trumpet. Another blast and the headless guy disappears.

"What about self-destructive impulses?" The doctor covers up a yawn.

"Like what?" I want him to come right out in English and say what he means.

"Burning or cutting yourself." I shake my head. "But you have had those impulses in the past?" I do feel something when I hear the word *burning*. I may have been burning before the world caught fire.

"What about suicidal thoughts?" He yawns again. "Are you having those?"

I stand up. I want to leave now. "No, I'm not," I say, "but if I have to stay here much longer and answer your questions, I'll probably start."

He puts down his pencil. He may look at me then. I can't see well enough to tell.

5

ATTITUDE

THE NURSE TRACKS ME DOWN IN the T.V. Lounge where I'm listening to a cooking show. I hear things sizzling. "Mmmm," the cook says. She has a woman's voice. "Look at the colours! Red peppers. Purple eggplant. Green zucchini."

She loses me there. They all sound the same in the frying pan.

"How long have I been here?" I ask the nurse. He wants me to call him Morris, but I'm not ready to be on a first name basis with him.

"In 5B?" he says. "Just over a week. And a while before that in 3A."

"I was in another building?"

"When you came in. Medium Security. You really impressed them there, kicking a nurse and trying to fly out through a window. They had a suicide watch on you for a few days. Is this yours?" He holds up a grey T-shirt.

I squint at it. "I don't know. What does it say on the front?"

"Blackstone Village Volunteer Fire Department. I found it in a box down in the laundry room. I thought I remembered you came in from around there."

I like the idea of grey. It's an in-between colour that keeps its voice down and whispers.

I also realize I like the idea of coming from somewhere.

I hold out my hand. The nurse gives me the shirt, and after that, my meds. It isn't just the H. pill I take. There's also a green one to control some of the tremor H. causes. And a yellow pill to take away the side effects of the green one.

They can't do anything about my eyes yet.

I swallow all the meds down with water while the nurse watches. Then I open my mouth to show him I'm not hiding a pill or two in between my teeth and my cheek or under my tongue.

"You're not a bad kid," he says. "Can I give you a word of advice?"

It's another rhetorical question.

"When you see the doctor," he goes on, "try to act motivated. You know what that means?"

"Finally a question I know the answer to," I say.

The nurse shakes his head. "Now see, that's the kind of attitude I'm talking about. You don't act like you're serious about getting better. Listen to me." He leans in closer.

"There are a lot of lost people here. They all need help. If you don't give a damn, the doctor won't either. He'll send you out at the end of the month with some pills and a prescription.

"Who knows what will happen to you after that?"

6

Fitting In

The first day I have cafeteria privileges, I walk over for lunch, get a sandwich, bottle of pop and sit down at a table by myself. In a while someone sets a tray piled high with what to my limited vision looks like road kill on the table and sits down beside me.

"How are you feeling," he asks. His voice is a little childish. Popsicles and candy on a stick.

"Like I've been through hell," I say.

There's a pitcher of water on the table. I try to pour some in a glass. My hand shakes so badly I can't hold it. He does it for me. Or it could be the headless man standing behind him.

"Howard means are you happy being here?" the guy with the little-kid voice says.

"You're kidding." I look around to see if he's talking about the headless man, but he's disappeared.

"The food's good here," little-kid voice goes on. "You have a bed at night with no bed bugs. Nobody tries to steal your stuff like they do at the men's hostel. And they don't kick you out during the day."

He eats while he talks. Between his hands and his mouth it's a blur, although it would be to me, anyway.

"Say yes to the suicide question," he tells me.

"Which question?"

"The suicide question. Doctors are more inclined to keep you past the thirty days if you say you're suicidal."

"Too late," I say.

He sets down his knife and fork. "Howard's sorry. He should have told you sooner."

"It's okay," I say. "I'm not really keen to stay."

He picks up his silverware and starts to eat again, but when he's finished he asks, "Do you have a place to go?"

"No."

"Any family to help you out?"

"Not that I know of."

"You should stay here as long as possible then. Tell them you'll cut your wrists if they send you out. It might work a time or two, until they catch on."

He gets up and goes past the food line and into the kitchen. When he comes back he's carrying a bowl of chocolate pudding. "Last week's," he says. "The cook used to be a patient here. She saves it for Howard."

"I'm confused," I say. "Are you the Howard you keep talking about?"

He acts like he hasn't heard me. "What's your name?"

"No idea."

"You're a John Doe?" He clucks his tongue. "Do you have a diagnosis yet?"

"Do I need one?"

The guy I've decided is Howard leans his elbows on the table. "That's why the doctors are asking you all those questions. They go through this book until they find the name that goes with what you have and then," he snaps his fingers, "bingo!"

"Bingo what?"

"Bingo they know what to call you. And where you fit in."

"What if I don't fit anywhere?"

Howard seems to think this over for a minute. "Then you'll have to be careful," he says, "because they'll make you fit. It's their job."

7

BINGO

I DON'T MEET WITH THE SNEEZING doctor the next time. It's a different one. Dr. Charon. He's a bobble-head. As soon as I sit down in his office he says, "I have reason to believe your name may be Dan. Does that sound familiar?"

This doctor has the kind of voice you get when you suck the helium out of a balloon. He waits for my answer.

I've decided to take the nurse's advice and cooperate. I've also decided I'd like to be somebody, even if that's not who I really am. I answer, "Well, I've definitely heard the name before."

"So you feel you might be Dan?"

"Dan." I say the word out loud and nod my head. "I feel it's . . . familiar."

"Do you have any idea what your last name might be, Dan?"

I don't of course, but being in limbo is not that comfortable. I think I may be ready for one. "I've . . . ," I say

"Yes?" The doctor jumps right in. It looks like he wants me to have a name, too.

"I think that I've . . . er . . . "

"ly? You're saying Iverly. Is that it?"

"Maybe." I take my time. "Yes," I say. "I think it could be."

"That's confirmation!" His pen dances across the notebook on his desk. "First name Dan." He writes as he talks. "Last name Iverly. Middle name or initial unknown."

His hand comes up. I see a flash of something — maybe light hitting a ring on one of his fingers. He sits back in his chair, I think a happy man.

I also feel happy about the way things have gone. It's obvious you need some kind of label in this world I'm in. Now I have one.

"I wasn't sure whether or not to believe her when your cousin — " the doctor pauses. I think he's glancing down at his desk, "Matti came in looking for you. You remember Matti?"

I don't. "Matti . . . ?" I say. My brain is slow. I've already forgotten my last name.

"Iverly. Your cousin. I had some doubt about her story, I'll admit. Then I had a call from the person in charge of Emergency Social Services in Kingman confirming what she told me. Now you're confirming what I learned from him.

"Everything's beginning to fit together. I'll have to see if the story checks out, of course. But we're very far behind on the paper work. So many lost people coming out of the fire. I'm willing to accept Dan Iverly as your name."

His chair squeaks like rusty nails on glass as he swivels back and forth. "I can see how it happened. You're visiting family. You go out hiking. Not a smart idea, but you get lost somewhere in the fire area. No food. No water. You fall, perhaps. Hit your head. And bingo."

I believe I've heard the magic word. "That's my diagnosis?" I ask.

"Yes," he says. "In layman's terms I believe it is." He sits forward and begins to write again. "You've had a psychotic break brought on by severe stress. Keep taking your meds and with any luck you'll make a complete recovery."

"And without luck?" I ask. "Also in layman's terms."

"But you are lucky. You were lost. Now you're found. End of story."

8

Corpse Moss

HOWARD'S PLEASED WHEN HE HEARS I'M not a John Doe anymore. But he doesn't like the diagnosis. "Psychotic break?" he says. He sticks out his lower lip and shakes his head. "Anyone could have that. It's nothing you can take to the bank, is it?"

Still he suggests we celebrate. "When you get your first day pass, we should take the bus in to Kingman for cokes and hot wings. My treat."

"When will that be?" I ask.

"How long have you been here?"

"I haven't had a conversation with a watch since I came in," I say, "so I wouldn't know."

Howard promises to find out. Then he's not around for a few days and I still don't know about the day pass.

I miss Howard. The better I get, the harder it is to find things to do with my time.

I still can't read. And I've given up listening to cooking shows. How much frying and boiling can a guy take? My hands shake too much to be any good at stick hockey. I have the same problem with the activities in handicrafts.

A lot of people smoke for something to do. That's not attractive to me at this point. I also don't have any money.

Sitting and walking in circles is about all there is to do outside. Sports equipment is banned, I suppose for obvious reasons. I might take a baseball bat and attack another patient. Or turn it on myself. That's assuming I have the energy to pick it up to begin with.

They do have a beauty shop at the hospital. On a whim I go in there. "Want a hair cut?" a girl asks. She tells me her name is Angie.

I run my hands over my head. "It's not too far away from a pig shave now," I say.

"I could dye it for you," Angie tells me. "I've heard a change can be as good as a rest."

Is corpse moss an actual colour? That's how I'd describe my hair when she finishes with it. Hopefully she'll take a few more classes at her beauty school in Kingman before she works on anybody else.

I look in the mirror and see a dead person looking back at me. He's not headless. I haven't seen that guy in a while. "Get lost!" I say.

Angie thinks I'm talking to her. "Sorry," she says. "The dye kind of got away on me. Want me to buzz your hair right off?"

"No thanks," I tell her.

"A few piercings would perk you up. I'm not allowed to do piercings here. But when you get out?"

I shake my head. I've been pierced enough.

9

Going Up

THERE'S A BENCH OUT IN FRONT of the cafeteria I sometimes sit on. Howard finds me there one day and tells me I have to move. "This is why I still volunteer at the hospital," he clucks, "even though I'm not a patient anymore." He points above his head. "Look how cloudy it's getting. If the sky falls this is a dangerous place to be."

I'm not in the mood to argue so I move farther back by the edge of an abandoned brick building. I stretch out on the dead grass and look up at the sky. Howard sits down beside me.

The clouds are all cumulus — the puffy kind little kids look at and see birds or small animals in. "I remember hearing a story about the sky falling," I tell Howard. "Something lands on Chicken Little's head. I believe it's an acorn. Chicken Little thinks it's the sky and runs around telling everybody. Goosey Loosey. Turkey Lurkey. All the friends rhyme."

"Howard loves that story," he says. "But Chicken Little doesn't think the sky's falling. He knows it is. He and his friends go to tell the king."

"Then the fox eats them all at the end."

Howard snorts. "There is no fox in Howard's version. Chicken Little keeps warning people about the sky. The end."

"You're serious?"

I squint at Howard. I must do it sceptically because he says, "I suppose you've heard of tornadoes?"

"I have."

"Well . . . " He smiles and I hear cotton candy winding around a paper stick. "Since I've been working here, a tornado has never touched down."

He stops talking and looks over his shoulder. "Do you know those folks over there?" He points at a couple of people by the cafeteria.

"Sorry," I say. "I can't see that far."

"Try," he says.

"You try. Put Vaseline on your eyeballs first."

"I'll look for you, then," Howard says.

"There's a girl. She has short, dark hair and a round face. I've seen her here before. She kind of shines." He holds up his hand and waves.

"There are two men with her, both wearing black baseball caps. One's taller. The other man's hurt somehow, but . . . I'd say getting better and . . . " He waves again. "You told me you didn't have any family."

"I said I don't know of any. Please quit waving," I tell him. "They're probably do-gooders who want to save our souls."

Howard goes toward the people he's been staring at like he hasn't heard me. "Come on, Dan," he says. "I think they're here to see you."

Eventually I get up and follow him.

"Are you Dan?" the taller man asks. He steps around Howard. I squint at him. "Dan Iverly?" he asks again.

"He is." Howard pokes me in the ribs.

"Oh," I say. "Yes. I guess I am."

"You guess?"

"No," Howard says. "He knows he is."

"Then I guess that makes me your uncle Frank." The tall man holds out his hand. My own are shaking so much I've put them in my pockets to hold them down. I take the right one out now. It's moving like a tiny room fan. He clamps on to it and for a moment solves the problem.

I think he asks me a question then. What system am I from? Do I say, "The Milky Way?" Or do I just keep that in my head?

"This is Marsh," Frank says, meaning the other man standing in his shadow. "I understand he took care of you while you were in Blackstone Village, living in my office." He lists all the jobs he holds there, then adds, "But I'm down in Kingman now helping out with emergency relief."

A couple of times while he's talking I feel like I'm floating above everyone else. I want to comment on that. I want to tell them I have an elevator for a soul.

"Going up!" I want to sing out. But I keep my teeth together.

The man he's introduced steps into the sunlight. I don't remember him either but I haul my hand out of my pocket again. "Hello," I say.

Does he shout, "Run for cover?"

No, I think he says something about recovering. That I am.

There's an awkward pause after that. Then Frank turns, looks behind him and leads someone forward. "And this," he says, "is Matti."

I can't place the person who steps toward me, but she hums with energy. It's robin's egg blue. "Here," she says. She reaches something out to me. It's a ring on a silver chain. When she puts it in the palm of my hand it feels like water.

We all go to the cafeteria to drink cokes and eat big pieces of white cake that taste like air. I continue to squint. "I'm sorry," I say. "I can't see very well. The medication I'm on blurs my vision."

"We thought maybe you needed specs," Frank says. He and Marsh laugh high up in their chests.

"I'm sorry," I say again.

"Nothing to be sorry about," Frank tells me. "Not that I know of anyway."

I put both hands around my glass of coke, leave it on the table and bend over so I can drink with a straw. I'm afraid if I pick the glass up, I'll break it.

We're quiet after that. I probably have things in my head I want to say, but when everyone gets ready to leave, I can't recall any of them.

Matti turns and looks at me.

"Thank you for the ring," I tell her. "Did you buy it for me?"

"No," she says. "It's yours. But you can't keep the chain. That still belongs to me."

10

FUDGE

WHEN HOWARD'S NOT AROUND I SOMETIMES sit out in front of the hospital administration building and listen to the cars that pull up there. You never have to second-guess the condition they're in. They're always pretty honest about it. Trucks are the same. And buses.

A bus pulls up while I'm there. Proud diesel engine idling like dark chocolate. People get off the bus and walk toward me. One of them stops and hands me a small, plastic bag.

"Here," she says. It's Matti. I recognize her by the way she hums.

I open the bag and right away I know what's in it — *know* in this case means *remember*. My nose remembers. My mouth remembers. My stomach.

Million Dollar Fudge.

"Eat it if you want," Matti says. She sits down on the other end of the bench. Her hum moves into a higher gear.

I take a bite of fudge — just one bite, and there's a reconnection somewhere in my brain.

"You can talk with your mouth full," she says. "I don't care."

I would talk with a mouthful. It's clear Matti expects me to. But there's so much going on inside my head. Rockets launching. Comets snapping their tails as they whiz by. A new galaxy opening up. And then there's the luscious, velvet sounding taste of what I've just put in my mouth.

"Slow down," I caution myself. "Breathe." But I can't stop myself. I eat another piece.

"It didn't seem like you remembered me when I was here before," Matti says. "Marsh, either. He took care of you, too."

"I remember some things," I say around the planetarium-show in my mouth. "I usually can't tell if they actually happened."

"We put too much pressure on you the other day. I should just have come alone."

Matti talks about someone named Bee. A friend. Do I remember her? I shake my head, although the name might be familiar. She carries on with a string of questions like that while her voice gets farther and farther away. Or I do.

I'm on some kind of chocolate nirvana high. Smoke comes and goes. Fire. Demons. Water. Names. Ravens fly into my life and fly away again. They talk. They don't talk. Lights and ghosts fade.

Am I remembering? I don't know if that's what I'm doing. But if someone put a microphone in my face right then and asked me to comment on the experience, I'd says Matti's fudge should be served to patients in mental hospitals all across the country. It has done more to clear the smoke from my brain than all the green and yellow and alphabetical pills I've taken since I got here.

I'm not a doctor of course. And I'll continue to take their advice. But I will give this testimonial: by the time Matti leaves, the vision in my left eye is almost back to normal.

11

THE FIRE

HOWARD HAS A THEORY ABOUT MEMORY. If something happens to you, that's traumatic, he says — something so big it hits you in the head and knocks you unconscious — your brain sticks it somewhere dark and puts a stone on top of it.

But this thing your brain is hiding from you will keep trying to come out, he says, so you end up using more and more of your energy to hold the stone in place. You do that because if the stone rolls away, all that painful stuff it was sitting on will come bursting out. And that can be almost as bad as whatever happened to you in the first place.

I don't know where Howard learned this. He may have made it up. It isn't what happens to me. There's no explosion when my memory starts to come back. No sudden blast of lightning.

It's more like what happens when you dig a hole in the sand at the seashore. It's completely empty when you're finished, but if you check back in a few minutes, water is already seeping back in.

I can't say for sure it was Matti's fudge that got me started, but hour by hour, drop by drop, my sorry life started to come back to me.

I'd be walking outside. I'd look down at my feet and I'd see the shoes I used to wear. They had pointed toes and the sides came up and buckled around my ankles.

"Queer boots," my father used to call them.

Or I'd be lying in bed in my room at the hospital and suddenly I'd be in the room I had in his house. I won't use the word *home*. It was never like that.

I'd remember how I kept all my books hidden under the bed because when he was sober my father thought reading anything but the Bible lead to a relationship with the devil. He put anything he found in the fire.

Then when he was drunk, he was the fire.

He never laid a hand on me, but he let me know that nothing I did would ever be good enough. Over and over I heard that I was evil. Perverse. A blot on the family name.

I have the same dream several nights in a row. I want it to be a dream. I'm high up on an outcropping of rock. I take out my wallet and begin to pull things out of it. My school card. My library card. My driver's license.

I can read my name clearly on each one of them. It's not Dan Iverly.

One at a time, I send these cards spinning away from me and down into the gorge below. "I don't have a name any more!" I scream. "Now I'm nobody."

After a while the dream is also with me during the day.

And then it's not a dream at all. It's my life.

I want to talk to Howard, but he's suddenly not around. I try to talk to my nurse instead. I even call him by his name. "Morris," I say, "I have a problem. Can we sit down and talk?"

Morris is pushing his pill cart around. In the past there have been thefts so he won't move two inches away from it. "Only one?" he says. "You're a lucky guy."

"I don't feel lucky," I tell him.

"You are." Morris reaches into his pocket. "I've got a day pass here for you. Take the bus into town. You can even have an over-night on the weekend."

"I don't have anywhere to go."

"Try the library," he says. "Have a coffee. Things are turning out well for you, so enjoy yourself."

When Howard saunters up to me later that day he already knows about the pass. "Perfect timing," he says. "We'll go to the King's Roost in Kingman tomorrow. They have a happy hour special there. Hot wings for twenty-five cents each. You'll love it."

"There's something I need to talk to you about," I say.

"Tomorrow," Howard says. "Happy hour's a perfect time to talk."

12

WINGS

WE PICK A BOOTH IN THE corner of the King's Roost where it's quiet and we can talk. The waitress comes over chewing gum and smiling at the same time. "Boys," she says. "I'm Crystal." She pops her gum. If she's a day older than Howard, I'll be surprised. "What can I getcha?"

Howard takes three dollars out of his pocket and plunks them on the table. "Let's have a dozen hot wings," he says.

Crystal stops chewing her gum. "A pitcher to go with that?"

"Two diet cokes," Howard says. "No ice." When she goes back to the kitchen he tells me proudly. "I come here a lot. I'm probably one of their best customers."

We don't have to wait long before the wings arrive. I eat two and Howard vacuums up the rest. Crystal comes back when there's nothing on the table except empty glasses and a pile of bones.

"Anything else?" she says. She's irritated about something. When she pops her gum it sounds like she's shooting B. B.'s.

Howard puts down three more dollars. "The same again, please," he says. "And can you make them hotter? Like, you do call them *hot wings*."

"The manager wants me to remind you that it's happy hour," Crystal says. "He'd like you to have a beer each, at least."

"That's very nice of him," Howard says. "Tell him thank you, but we're both on medication. We can't drink. And we're happy already."

From the way she yanks her long hair back off her face, it's easy to tell Crystal isn't happy. Not even close.

We wait quite a while for the next order of wings and cokes. Long enough that I imagine they've had to scour the neighbourhood for more chickens. It gives me a chance to talk to Howard. "What I wanted to tell you," I say, "is that Matti's not my real cousin."

"You could have fooled me," Howard says.

"And Dan's not my real name."

"What about the other one?"

"Iverly? That's not mine, either."

"Well," Howard's taken all the plastic containers of jam out of their metal rack and now he's stacking them. When he's built them up high enough that they fall over, he looks at me the way I imagine the king would have looked at Chicken Little, if he'd made it all the way to the castle. Or she had.

"Do you know what your real name is?" he asks.

"I'm afraid so," I say.

"That means you have more names than you can use. You'll have to get rid of one."

"I've already tried that," I say. "It didn't work."

Howard begins putting all the jam containers back in their support structure. "Which name do you like best?" he asks me.

"Dan Iverly," I say. "I don't want anything to do with the other one."

"You're Dan to me then," he says. The jams are all back in their rightful places. He rests.

"But I have to tell someone my legal name, don't I?" I ask. "I at least have to tell Frank and Matti"

"Why?" Howard asks. "You're not hurting anybody. Hasn't your life been complicated enough already?"

The new wings arrive. I taste one and reach for my coke. "My God!" I gasp. "What's in these? Gun powder?"

Howard's face is flaming. Beads of sweat appear on his upper lip. I hear them popping out like corks from tiny bottles of champagne. "They are pretty hot," he says.

When he's on his fifth or sixth wing, he begins to wheeze and Crystal suddenly appears. "Beer?" she asks. "It'll coat your throat."

Howard waves her away and runs to the bathroom with tears running down his face.

"Are you trying to burn us alive?" I ask her.

"Don't blame me," she says. She blows a day-glow bubble. "I'm not the cook."

I get up and follow Howard into the bathroom.

When we come out again, a small, sharp-faced man is waiting for us by the cashier's desk. I'm guessing he's the manager. "Who's paying for the cokes?" he asks. I can see the tips of his eyeteeth when he talks.

Howard's face is puffy and pink-streaked. He's got a rattle in his chest. He looks ill and shocked and basically like someone has attacked him. But this little snotty man is worried about money for cokes?

I'm suddenly as angry as you can get when you're on medication to even out your emotions. "Who's paying for the hole in his throat?" I say.

"He asked for heat and he got it," the manager tells me. "Cokes are three dollars each during happy hour. That's twelve dollars you owe me." He holds out his hand.

"What?" Howard says. "Cokes are supposed to be free during happy hour." He fumbles around in his pockets until I tell him to stop.

"The cokes are on the house," I say. I look at the manager. He might as well be my father standing there. He *is* my father for just a second. "Otherwise I'm reporting you for having rats in your bathroom."

"What?" He whispers because people are looking our way. "There are no rats in my restaurant."

"Two big rats," I say, louder than before. "I just saw them when I was in the bathroom." I pull Howard toward the door. "And there's another rat by the cash register," I yell as I close the door behind us.

"Cokes are supposed to be free during happy hour," Howard says when we're on the bus again. "And Howard thought they liked him there."

"It's just the manager," I tell him. "I think the waitress liked you." I don't say, "I think the waitress liked Howard." I've decided to talk to him the way I would anyone else.

"She did?" The woman across the aisle from us hands Howard a Kleenex so he can blow his nose.

"Well enough," I say. "But maybe it's time for you to find a new place to be happy."

Howard rides back to the hospital with me. "It's my responsibility he says. I was your sponsor while you were in town." He leaves after that and I get a phone call from Matti.

She's found out I have a weekend pass coming up. She wants me to spend it in Kingman. "It will be like a reunion," she says. I'll get Frank and Marsh to come down from the village. Frank needs to talk to you, anyway."

The last part sounds ominous, but I agree to go.

13

WELCOME

WHEN I MEET MATTI AT THE main terminal in town, I look like I've been on a three-day drunk. The electric razor Morris let me use has sharp holes in the mesh cover. I have scraps of toilet paper stuck on all the nicks I made in my skin. My hair has faded to something you could call puke-brown And the shirt I'm wearing isn't as clean as I thought it was when I put it on.

Matti still seems genuinely glad to see me. She doesn't even mention my appearance.

We board another bus together, then get off and start up a steep sidewalk that takes us to the place Matti calls *the palace.* After about a block and a half, I need to stop and get my breath.

Matti stops with me. She shields her eyes to look at something farther up toward the top of the hill. "Do you see her?" she says.

"Who?" I say.

"It's Mrs. Stoa," Matti says. "She's been anxious to meet you. I guess she couldn't wait."

We work our way up slowly as the lady in question works her way down. "What took you so long?" she calls when she's still half a block away.

"Life," Matti calls back.

Mrs. Stoa is very small, but even with my one good eye I still couldn't miss her. She's wearing something long and bright green. A coat maybe? A long dress? And there's a band of gold standing out wide around her face.

She's slightly out of breath when we meet up. So am I.

"What have you got on?" Matti asks the lady.

"My good coat," the lady says. "And hat." She tips the gold band further back from her face. "Introduce me, please."

"Mrs. Stoa," Matti sighs, "I'd like you to meet my cousin, Dan Iverly."

Mrs. Stoa tilts her head back to look at me. "So you've made your way through, Dante," she says. Her voice is antique silver. "You're younger than your namesake, but still I knew you would."

She holds her hand out to me. It's tiny. The fingers are slightly curled.

"Welcome."

14

Beatrice

The place we're staying is large enough to hold the population of a small country. When we get there Mrs. Stoa excuses herself to take a nap, and Matti shows me my room. It's upstairs, at the opposite end of the hall from hers.

"I'll hang out here for a while," I say. "If it's okay." It's taken a lot for me to get here and I'm exhausted.

The room is quiet. There's just the sound of birds outside in the tree branches. At one point I think I can make out a face in among them. I let it be.

I go back downstairs just before five. Matti's pulled stools up around a counter in the middle of the kitchen. She's set out place mats, candles and wine glasses. "I can't drink with this medication," I tell her.

"I'm not old enough to drink," she says. "But I think the glasses look fancy."

"They do," Mrs. Stoa says. She steps into the kitchen yawning. Holds her hand up against her ear like she might hear things herself. "Am I supposed to do something?"

"Maybe go back upstairs and take off your bathrobe," Matti says.

"This is not a bathrobe." Mrs. Stoa makes a wobbly turn in front of the refrigerator. "It's a caftan. And I was referring to something I was supposed to do about dinner."

"I've ordered pizza," Matti says. She looks at me and rolls her eyes. "It's supposed to come right at six. Frank will be here by then and he can pay for it."

The doorbell rings. It's the pizza delivery guy. He comes in with three boxes, each inside its own red thermal envelope.

"You're an hour early," Matti tells him. "My father isn't here yet with his credit card."

The delivery guy shifts his attention to the only other male in the room. "Don't look at me," I say. He does, anyway.

I pull my pockets inside out to show him all I have in either one is holes. He starts to pack up the pizza boxes again.

"Just a moment," Mrs. Stoa says. "My nephew will have a card at King Koffee we can use. You," speaking to the pizza guy, "will drive this young woman down the hill to get the card in question. You will leave the pizza here."

"But . . . " he says.

"Matti will be your security." He gapes at her. "Hostage then, if that's clearer to a person your age."

We sit in the living room while we wait for Matti to come back. The pizzas are staying warm in the oven until everyone gets here. Our delivery guy insisted on taking his thermal envelopes back with him.

"You must be hungry," Mrs. Stoa says. She sets down a bowl of something that looks like breakfast cereal on the coffee table between us. "Bits and Bobs," she says. "I make it myself."

Bits and Bobs actually is cereal, as near as I can tell — two or three kinds, with nuts and pretzels thrown in. I take a handful and fill my mouth.

"Lots of food value in this," Mrs. Stoa says. She picks out a piece of something square and puts it in her mouth. "Vitamins in the cereal. Protein in the nuts."

She watches me while I take more. "That's an interesting ring you're wearing. Where did you get it?"

I look down at the snake ring on my thumb. "I don't have any idea," I say. That's the complete truth.

"Matti found it on the beach the day you left. Did you know she thought it was a sign you'd decided to take your own life?"

I shake my head. It's a little hard to swallow after hearing that.

"I have always felt things would work out for you," Mrs. Stoa says, "since I first heard of your arrival and saw your face. But you will have to seize this opportunity." She leans forward and looks at me intently. "My given name is Beatrice. Does that mean anything to you?"

"Well . . ." I've given up on the Bits and Bobs. "Does it have something to do with . . . "

"Your story?" She nods. "You'll understand it all in time."

I definitely don't understand it now, but I have the feeling she wants something more from me. "Are you saying you . . . do you want me to call you Beatrice?"

"Certainly not," she says. She plucks some of my letters out of the air. The B, E and A. The T. The R. She leaves I, C and E glistening between us. It takes a while for them to melt.

15

Butter Brickle

Matti gets back just before Frank arrives. Marsh comes in after them. Another minute later, Chuck joins us. He owns the palace, apparently. Or his father does. We finally eat.

Mrs. Stoa wants candles lit and the lights turned off to create what she calls, "the proper atmosphere." I think she intends for us to eat slowly and engage in conversation.

The reverse happens. Nobody seems to feel like talking in the dark so it's all loud chewing and swallowing and grunting. At one point Matti says, "Yuck! What this little fishy thing?"

"Anchovy," Frank says. He and Marsh reach for it with their forks at the same time.

When there's nothing left but salad, Chuck leaves to go back to work. Frank stands up, stretches and says, "I think I'll go out and get us some ice cream."

"I'll come with you." Marsh pushes back from the table. "And then I have to hit the road back home."

"I thought I'd take Dan with me," Frank tells him. "I'd appreciate it Marsh, if you'd stay here and help Matti clean up."

Frank may be the mayor and whatever of Blackstone Village. He looks like an explosives expert to me. I'm expecting him to drop a bomb on me in the car, but all he does is light a small firecracker.

"Matti's got her heart set on you coming back to the village when you get out," he says before he starts the engine. "There's work for you to do. Mostly pick and shovel to start with, but Marsh won't push you too hard until you get your bearings. He knows more than you think about your situation."

"I could probably do pick and shovel," I say.

"Probably?" He eyes me suspiciously. I'm still expecting him to light the fuse that will blow me apart.

"I could," I say. "Definitely."

Frank runs his hands back and forth over the steering wheel cover. "Somehow you've managed to convince my daughter you're a good person. She's usually right about such things. All the same . . . "

"I would never hurt Matti," I say."

"I know you wouldn't. Not if you valued your life." He turns the key in the ignition and I break out in a sweat.

Too much firepower in the car and most of it isn't mine.

When we're standing in front of the counter at the ice cream store, Frank says, "You care for butter brickle?"

"I don't know," I say.

He asks the girl who's waiting on us to give me a taste. It isn't like Matti's fudge, but it's sweet with a lot of crunch. Frank buys a quart.

We sit for a minute after we get into his car, both of us facing forward. Then Frank turns and looks at me. "I found out something about your past," he says.

"My what?" I start to sweat again.

"I . . . " Frank hesitates. He actually seems embarrassed. "I got hold of your fingerprints. I sent them in to someone who owes me a favour. I know who you are."

This is more like the bomb I was expecting, although it's not just a bomb. It's a stealth missile. "You got my fingerprints?" I croak. "How did you manage to do that?"

"Marsh went back to the cafeteria and took the glass you were drinking from that day we visited." I put my head down in my hands. "Look," he turns toward me. "I'm not apologizing for doing that. It's part of how we clean up after a disaster like this one. And I thought you'd be glad to know."

"I'm not," I say. "And I already knew."

"You've remembered your name?" Frank says.

I nod. "And a lot more."

"Were you planning on telling anyone? Matti, at least?"

"No," I say. "I wasn't. I planned to go on being Dan Iverly and start a new life. But you can relax, Frank. I get it."

The butter brickle is on the seat between us. I pick it up. "You wanted to make sure I'm not an axe murderer. Now you know, but you've still decided you don't want a screw-up like me associated with the family name."

Frank's mouth falls open. "You think that's what this is about?"

"I do. I think you don't want me calling myself Dan Iverly because it will embarrass you socially." The ice cream is beginning to make my hands feel cold.

"Hells bells," Frank says. "There's nothing precious about my name. You can change yours legally to Iverly any time you want since you're over eighteen. You don't need my permission. You go back a hundred years though, and you'll probably find you're sharing it with horse thieves."

He turns away and we sit a while. "Before you were talking about giving me a job up where you live," I say eventually. "Have you changed your mind about that?"

"Matti's got her heart set on it, like I said."

"I'll take the job then, as long as you agree to keep what you found out about me between us."

"All right." Frank shrugs and starts the car. "But I don't see why you're so hush-hush about the whole thing. From what I found out, you have nothing to be ashamed of."

16

A Little Guy with Suspenders

Howard isn't around the day I leave the hospital. After I've looked everywhere else I can think of, I go to the cafeteria and knock on the kitchen door. A guy with a neck too thin for his Adam's apple opens it. "I'm looking for the cook who's a friend of Howard's," I say.

"Howard?" The guy seems to reflect on the name for a minute. "He work here?"

"Not in the kitchen," I say. "But I thought he had a friend here who saved food for him. He said she used to be a patient herself."

The guy must be a cook. He has something white all over his hands and his apron. It occurs to me that he might be the one who makes the air cake they serve in the cafeteria.

"Edith, you mean?" he says. "Yeah. She was always giving food to people. That's why she doesn't work here anymore."

"She's not around at all?"

"No, she's gone. And don't ask me for a handout, because I can't do it."

"I wasn't going to," I say. Obviously. I have both my hands in my pockets. "It's not her I want, anyway. I'm trying to find the guy she used to give food to. Howard, like I said."

"Can't help you there," The cook says. He closes the door. White powder flies up into the air.

I go back to 5B and ask for Howard there. "The little guy with the rainbow suspenders," I tell people. They all nod when they hear the description, but that's as far as it goes.

When I walk out the door of the Metal Springs Hospital late that afternoon and get into Marsh's truck, I feel positive about everything I'm about to do, except leaving without telling Howard goodbye.

That doesn't seem right after all he's done for me.

17

PARADISE

WE MAKE SEVERAL STOPS FOR SUPPLIES on the way to Blackstone Village. We also stop at a burger place to eat, so it's dark by the time we arrive. Marsh lets me off in front of the little egg-shaped trailer he says is my new home.

He gets out of his truck and opens the door. "You're just behind Frank's house," he says. "I ran a cord over from there to give you power." He flips a switch and a lamp comes on.

In two seconds I've looked all around me.

"This okay?" Marsh asks. "Frank thought you should have your own place."

I sit on the narrow bed that runs across the fat end of the trailer. "Where's Matti?" I ask.

"You probably won't be seeing much of her for a while." Marsh leans against the door frame. "She stays in her room all day. She says it's because she's bored but I don't think that's it. I think she isn't coping very well."

"Oh," I say. "I'm sorry."

"Like the man says, life ain't easy."

Marsh straightens up. "You've got water." He points at a jug on the tiny counter that runs across the front of the trailer. "Outhouse is up in the trees. Breakfast's at the Hot Spot across the way at six-thirty. Let's get some sleep." He opens the door and steps outside. "Good night."

I stay on the bed after he leaves and look around again. There are a few things I missed the first time. A dried flower in an old maple syrup bottle on the counter, for example. Books on a shelf above the bed. It's not quite the welcome I was hoping for, but it does look like somebody's expecting me.

I stay where I am until I hear a bell tinkling. I get up and look out the window over the counter. It's the only one in the trailer.

I can't see anything, but as the sound gets louder, I realize it's two bells I hear. One is like water running over rocks. The other is a plague bell. One that bongs, "Bring out your dead."

I'm not sure what kind of visitation to expect when I open my door, but it's Mrs. Stoa who is walking toward me with a flashlight in one hand and a bell in the other. Behind her is Matti. What she's carrying is the sound of a funeral.

"Marsh let you off here and didn't tell us?" Mrs. Stoa says. She shakes her head. "That boy never had any social skills, even before his war."

She climbs up the two steps to the trailer and stands in the doorway. Matti stays down on the ground. There really isn't room for three people inside.

"We just wanted to make sure you got settled in," Mrs. Stoa says. "And by the way, this trailer was Frank's idea. You can stay in the house if you'd rather."

Matti moves up on to the first step. She has something fuzzy and black on her head. It's pulled down so far over her ears that her face hardly shows.

"We have a bear in the area," she says.

"Oh, yes," Mrs. Stoa tells me. "If you go out at night for . . . any reason, ring this bell and make as much noise as possible. The bear will be as frightened of you as you are frightened of the bear."

She hands the bell to me. It's silver. Engraved with spirals and squiggly lines. "I'd like it back when the danger's past."

"It's a mother bear," Matti says. "She's grieving because of what she's lost."

"Perhaps," Mrs. Stoa says. "Did you find the books I left you?"

"Yes," I say. "Thank you."

"We'll leave you to them," she says. She waits for Matti to step down so that she can step down. Then they walk away.

I take the pills I brought with me from the hospital. One is supposed to help me shut my mind off and go to sleep. It really works. The bed is short and there's no room to hang my legs off the end so I have to curl my knees in to my stomach to fit, but I'm out in a few minutes.

I'm only disturbed once during the night. Something heavy heaves and scrapes against the side of the trailer. Something like a mother bear. "I wondered where you went," a candy-covered voice says. It almost sounds like Howard.

I can't answer because I'm asleep.

18

SCARS

IT'S STILL DARK WHEN I GET to the Hot Spot for breakfast. People are already lined up for whatever's coming off the grill. Pancakes, probably. The whole place is floating in maple syrup.

The guy lined up in front of me turns around. "Remember me?" he says. "I'm Virgil." He's handsome. Long hair. Dark eyes. But when I look at him, all I can think of are ravens.

"I'm the guy who went off and left you over in Cato City," he says. "Sorry about that." He steps back and looks me over. "Shorts and a T-shirt all you've got? It's cold in the mornings now." He takes his sweatshirt off and gives it to me. "Shirt off my back," he says. "There's gloves in the pocket. You're working with me today."

When Virgil and I come out of the Hot Spot, the sun's up and I see why Matti's not coping. It's like a scene from a World War II movie. There are huge piles of charred wood and rubble everywhere. Specks of black dust hang suspended in the air. Then the trucks roll in belching diesel and talking business.

In the time it takes us to pick up a chain saw and get into Virgil's old car, someone's loaded a burned-out school bus on a flat bed and is driving it away. And someone else — Marsh, probably, is wheeling back and forth in a bobcat, loading junk from the piles onto dump trucks.

Virgil drives the car to the far edge of town. He stops, gets out and takes the chainsaw out of the trunk. "Marsh went through here and took down most of the dead trees," he says. "We need to cut them into smaller pieces and pile them up so he can get at them with the bobcat. You ever use a chainsaw?"

"I doubt it," I say.

"I'll saw then, and you stack." He grabs a vest from the back seat of the car and walks a little distance away from me. When he starts up the saw, it's like I hear a pack of demonic wolves in the distance.

Then I realize it's the sound of something suffering. Trees, maybe. Who knows how long it takes a tree to die?

Lunch is back at the Hot Spot. I don't see Matti there. I don't see Frank. Mrs. Stoa puts in a brief appearance and reminds me of the importance of leafy green vegetables. When we're about finished eating, Marsh comes over.

He's wearing army camouflage with a Red Cross band on his arm. Or maybe I still can't trust me eyes completely. "How's it going?" he asks me. Then he looks at Virgil.

"We've been working flat out," Virgil says. He winks at me. "May have to slow down this afternoon."

We definitely do that. I'm tired after lunch from working. Virgil's more tired *of* working. We pick two fat logs to sit on. He pours out coffee from his thermos, and we take a long break in a clearing that was once thick with trees.

"It looks like you've had some serious burns on your legs," Virgil says. "How'd you come by those?"

By now I've accepted the fact that somewhere up in the mountains, I took the lit end of one cigarette after another and used it like a red-hot paint brush against my skin.

I tell him that. I figure I may as well be honest.

"Cigarettes'll kill you," Virgil says. "You need any help kicking the habit?"

"It's done," I say. "It wasn't too hard. I never actually inhaled."

19

BLUE BLAZES

SLEEPING IN *THE EGG*, AS MATTI calls my trailer, takes some getting used to. But I manage. The sounds that disturbed me get fainter every day. And I like being able to open the door and look out at the Milky Way.

I eat well. I get stronger. I can see how things will be better here next year and I want to be part of that. It still takes me a couple of weeks to decide the best way to make that happen.

Once I've decided I walk into the trailer where Frank has his temporary office and lay it out for him. "I want to change my name to Dan Iverly. Legally," I say. "I need to know you don't have a problem with that."

"I don't," he says. He's sitting behind his desk. Paper is piled up all over it and spills out onto the floor. "I told you that before."

He gives me that look again. Maybe he isn't suspicious. Maybe it's just a guy thing. "Matti says you're a Justice of the Peace."

"I am. But J.P.'s don't do name changes." I think I sag a little when he says that. "Move those insurance forms off the chair and sit down," he says. I carry out both orders.

"I'm also a Notary Public. I can notarize your statement saying you want to change your name from what it is now to something else. We'll fax that off to a person I know in the registry at Kingman. There's a fee, of course. But you're working now."

"You're sure I can do this?"

"Like I told you. You're over eighteen. You can change your name to Darth Vader if you want to."

I'm pretty sure my birthday is October 25, not that I was ever allowed to celebrate it. That's a little less than a month away according to the calendar in my trailer, so unless I've lost an entire year, my eighteenth birthday is coming up.

I don't know why Frank thinks I'm older than that. But I want to get started so I let it pass. "Okay," I say. "I'm ready."

Frank hands me a blank piece of paper and a pen. He tells me what to write. I hand it back to him when I'm finished.

"Now," he says. "I need you to swear to the truth of this. Raise your right hand." I do that, feeling self-conscious.

"Do you solemnly swear," he begins, "that what you have written here is true to the best of your knowledge? If yes, say I so solemnly swear."

I only get to, "I so sol…" when Frank cuts me off.

"Hold on," he says. "What did you write here?" He brings the paper closer to his face. "Eustace Aaron Miller?" His eyebrows soar up. It's almost like he has little black wings above each of his eyes.

"Are you crazy?" Right away I can tell he wishes he hadn't asked that. "You can't swear to this, I mean. You haven't put down your legal name."

"Yes, I have," I say.

"No, you haven't. You must still be confused."

"I'm not. Why would I make up a name like that?"

"Eustace Miller?" I can tell Frank's beginning to fizzle out.

"That's who I was. Useless Miller I was also called."

He shuffles through the papers on his desk. "Is this some kind of joke?"

"Not to me."

He finds a red folder, holds it up and opens it. "Your name, based on your fingerprints is Willis Asche."

"Who?" I ask.

"Asche, Willis Alan. Your parents had you finger-printed when you were eight as part of a missing child program. I've got it right here." Frank flaps the papers at me.

"I've never heard of him," I say.

Frank fiddles with the stapler on his desk. I think his time as an explosives expert is almost over.

"Listen, Frank," I say. Now it's my turn to lean forward. "I'm positive my father never had me fingerprinted for anything like a program to find missing children.

"I've always believed that if I was kidnapped, he'd yell, 'Amen,' and crack open a bottle of whiskey to celebrate."

"Your father's alive?" Frank's eyebrows go up again. The top layer of paper on his desk lifts slightly, then settles back down.

"As far as I know."

He studies the papers again. "This Willis Asche kid's whole family was killed in an automobile accident when he was nine. He was the only survivor. I've got a copy of the newspaper article here."

He pushes on his lips like he's searching for the switch that will make this whole problem go away. "You're positive about your dad?"

"I'm positive he didn't die when I was nine."

"And about the name? You didn't know what it was this time last month."

"Now I do."

"Son of a gun," Frank says. He slaps his hand down on the desk. Then he looks up at me. "If you're this Eustace Miller character, and it seems like you know what you're talking about, then who in blue blazes is Willis Asche?"

"I'm sorry, Frank," I say. "That name doesn't mean anything to me at all."

MATTI

1

Charcoal

I DECIDED THIS IS WHAT I'D tell a T. V. reporter if one ever stuck a microphone in my face and asked me, "Matti Iverly, what's it like to move back to the place you've lived all your life after it's been burned out?"

"If you're serious about finding out," I'd say, "get a bulldozer to come in and knock down most of the houses in your town. Make it your neighbourhood if you live in the city. Leave a few buildings standing for no reason you can understand.

"You can even let one of those buildings be your own house, if you're okay feeling guilty about having a roof over your head when your neighbours don't. Try living in your house while what's left of the ones around you have been bulldozed out.

"I wouldn't suggest setting your town or neighbourhood on fire before the bulldozer comes in," I'd add, "because fire can get away on you. You'll just have to dream up the smell of smoke and the black soot everywhere. You'll just have to imagine the feeling that your whole life has turned to charcoal."

Of course I'd be telling the T. V. reporter what it would be like for the average person to experience what I'd described.

For me? With my beloved Tourette's? Moving back to Blackstone Village turned out to be a hundred times worse than staying at the evacuation centre in Kingman, and not just because of the stuff I've already mentioned.

The sound of chainsaws and jackhammers and people shouting never seemed to stop during the day. Trucks constantly came and went. It was solid noise and confusion.

And there was no bus I could take to get away from all of it.

During the day, I wore the special kind of earmuffs jackhammer operators use. I stayed inside with the windows and doors shut and the curtains pulled. My main job was holding myself together. I barely managed that.

Even the mighty Mrs. Stoa had to back off on her advice-giving. And on the assignments she wanted me to do for school. I couldn't concentrate.

After dark, when all the work had stopped, I took off my earmuffs and sat in the porch swing. Dan visited me sometimes when I was there. We talked a little. But I wasn't very good company. And he was getting up early and working hard. He usually hit the hay by nine-thirty.

Virgil brought his guitar by a few times and checked in. He'd learned from Mrs. Stoa that he had a poet's name and he was trying to live up to it, so he wanted me to listen to a song he'd written for his new girlfriend.

I liked the quiet way he played. And his voice was not bad, but the song didn't have much in the way of lyrics — just, "Rosey, oh Rosey, oh," over and over again.

I told him he should put in something stronger, like, "Oh Rosey, I burn for you, babe." I showed him how that would sound, but he didn't go for it. "That's giving away too much," he said. "Jeez, Matti, I hardly know this girl."

At least he got my name right.

I would have stayed with my routine until every bit of burn was gone and the last nail was hammered into the new buildings that eventually went up. Routines work for me. They keep me from melting down.

A person like me doesn't get to sit on the sidelines much, though. It wasn't too long before I had to spring into action again.

2

OUT OF THE PHONE BOOTH

I WAS SITTING IN THE SWING out on the front porch one night
the way I usually did, when I heard Mrs. Stoa talking to someone
in the living room. "What on earth were you doing?" she said.
"Stealing that young man's fingerprints. Did you think you
were living in a detective novel?"

"Frank didn't take the glass." That was Marsh's voice. "I did."

Mrs. Stoa clucked her tongue. "Just like the two of you in
school. Frank egging you on and you covering for him."

I loved it when Mrs. Stoa talked about the two of them like
they were still kids in her class at high school. And this time I
definitely agreed with her.

I sat there swinging back and forth and eavesdropping. I
was actually enjoying myself for a change when another voice,
Frank's this time, snagged my attention.

"I thought at first my contact in Kingman had sent me the
results from the wrong fingerprints. I called and gave him an
earful. 'We're not rubes up here,' I said. 'We can tell when you've
sent us the wrong Intel.'

"He insisted he'd sent me the right results. I apparently sent
him the wrong fingerprints."

"My fault, Frank," Marsh said. I got up and moved close to the screen door.

"I suppose you involved Dan in this," Mrs. Stoa said. She clucked her tongue again.

I opened the door quietly and went through the hallway into the living room. All three of them were sitting there drinking tea. Mrs. Stoa was frowning. Frank's face was red and Marsh looked completely sheepish. "What's going on?" I said.

Then the truth came out about the whole ridiculous fingerprint-swiping episode. Dan finally remembering his name. And Frank insisting he was someone else.

"Dan could sue you for what you did," I said.

"No, he couldn't." Frank stuck out his chin. "It wasn't his fingerprints we took."

"I took them," Marsh said.

"Too bad we don't know who this Willis guy is," I said. "Then he could sue you both. And I'd make sure he did."

I went upstairs to bed, but I couldn't sleep. At first it was because I was so irritated at Frank and Marsh, but after a while I began getting curious about who the fingerprints actually belonged to. It turned in to a kind of puzzle for me.

There weren't that many people sitting at the table with us the day Frank and Marsh and I were at the Metal Spring hospital together. I closed my eyes and tried to remember exactly how it was.

It was just after three AM when I opened my eyes again. I switched on the radio in time to hear the tail end of the news. All of it was depressing. Murders. People getting blown up. Stock market information I couldn't imagine anybody being interested in.

At the end, the announcer did what they call a recap, where he reviewed everything you didn't want to hear in the first place. That's when I found out a tornado had touched down in a large city on the opposite side of the country.

No one was killed, but people were still in shock. "It came out of nowhere," a woman's voice said. "It sounded like a freight train was bearing down on us and then . . . " She was crying so she had to take a minute. "The whole world fell down on top of us."

It was the jog my memory needed. I sat up and looked at the clock. Only ten minutes since I looked the last time. Too early to go and wake Dan. I had to talk to him though. I was pretty sure by then I knew whose fingerprints Marsh had pinched.

Still, I was mature about it. I turned off the radio. I scrunched up the pillow behind my head. And I waited.

Just before five, I got up. I couldn't wear the earmuffs, because I wouldn't be able to hear what Dan had to say. Instead, I pulled a black toque as far down on my head as it would go, put on my jeans and a black turtleneck sweater with the collar turned up, and went outside and across to the egg.

I banged on the door, just like I used to when he was staying in the jail. Maybe a little louder. "Get up," I yelled. I banged a few more times before he called out, "What?" in a bleary voice.

"I have to talk to you ASAP," I said. I heard him fumbling around inside. Finally he stuck his head out the door.

"Matti," he said. "Wha . . . what do you want?" He was obviously only half awake. His face was puffy and he had a thermal-blanket print running up and down one side of his face.

"I know who this Willis guy is." I waited to let Dan take that in. He didn't seem to. "The guy whose fingerprints Marsh took," I said. "The one Frank thought was you." He was still acting very groggy.

"Meet me at the Hot Spot in five minutes. Arlen probably has some breakfast started. I'll get something for you."

"May I get dressed first?" Dan asked. "Or do you want me to come the way I am?"

I ignored that. "And hurry up. I don't want to be out too long after daylight."

By the time Dan got to Arlen's, I had coffee in take-out cups and some sausage rolls and cinnamon buns bagged up. We carried it all away from the Hot Spot and down toward the lake, close to the place Dan and I used to go when he first got here and I still called him the on-fire guy.

The sand was the same. The water, and the rocks. We were the ones who'd changed.

"You're a vampire now," Dan said. He bit into a sausage roll. "Is that why we need to do this so early? You have to get into your coffin as soon as the sun comes up?"

"I know all about the fingerprint mix-up," I said. "And I think I know who Willis Asche is." He kept on eating. "Do you want to know?"

"It doesn't really have much to do with me. He's some patient at the hospital I never met. Or maybe a visitor."

"Think about the people at our table," I told him. "The prints had to belong to one of them. I heard Marsh admit last night that he must have taken the wrong glass."

"Matti." Dan had been blowing on his coffee but now he took two or three swigs. "I was still out of it then, remember? And besides, I couldn't see very well."

"That's a good point," I said, "so just listen. We were sitting at a long table. Frank and Marsh were next to each other. We sat across from them. I was on your left.

"Obviously it wasn't any of our fingerprints." I couldn't tell if Dan was paying attention or not.

"There were some women down at the end of the table to the left of me. They were very loud and they talked in a foreign language. It couldn't have been one of them, unless they'd had a sex change before the age of eight.

"That's how old Willis was when his fingerprints were taken. Even then, the women would be too old.

"The only other person I could think of for a long time was an even older man down across from them. It can't be him for the same reason."

Dan finished his coffee so I gave him mine. "The fingerprints belong to someone invisible. Is that what you're telling me?" He didn't seem to care for the idea.

"Now you're being stupid," I said. "There actually was another person on your right side. I didn't remember at first because I felt shy around you and I didn't look in your direction very often. But we had those huge pieces of white cake, remember?"

Dan nodded. "They tasted like air."

"Egg cartons," I thought. "Anyway, I was looking at your plate, noticing you hadn't eaten anything when some guy slid an empty plate in front of you and slid your plate with the cake on it back toward him.

"He had to lean far forward to do it and I saw the edge of something rainbow coloured running up and down his back. Like suspenders."

Dan turned and looked at me. "You're talking about Howard?" I nodded. "He wasn't there."

"Yes, he was. He was with you when I first saw you sitting outside. I think he tagged along with us when we went in to eat and got a free meal."

"That sounds like him," Dan said. He threw the crumbs from the bag out to some ravens that were perched on a rock. "But what difference does it make if he really is this Asche guy? Maybe he just made up his first name like someone else we know."

"Maybe," I said. "But don't you think it's weird that his name came back to us here?"

Dan got up and dusted the crumbs off his jeans. "What are you suggesting?" he said. "What is it you want to do?"

I could hear car doors slamming which meant people were coming to work. I stood up, too, and readjusted my toque so it came as far down as possible. "When work's over and I can stand to come out again, I'm going to talk to Frank. Will you come with me?"

"Why Frank?" Dan asked.

"He started this mess," I said. That wasn't really true. I'm not sure even now who started what. But I definitely needed Frank's help to clear it up.

3

LIGHTNING

JUST AFTER FOUR O'CLOCK, DAN AND I were in Frank's office. He was on the phone when we came in but he got off when he saw us. "Dan," he said. "Matti." He cocked his head at me. "Nice to see you in the daylight. Any particular reason for the getup?"

I didn't let him distract me. "When you first told me down in Kingman that you knew who Dan was, even though you didn't, you said his whole family was killed in a car accident. Right?"

"I think so," Frank said.

"How did you find out about that?"

"The . . . connection I have in Kingman sent me a copy of an old newspaper clipping about it."

"Do you have it?" I asked.

"Yes," he said.

"May we see it?" I was trying to keep things businesslike.

"I don't know where I put it," Frank mumbled. He hardly ever mumbled so it was a dead give-away that he was hiding something.

"What about that red folder over on the TV tray by your desk?" Dan asked. "That's where you had it when I was here before."

Frank made a show of noticing the folder and then picking it up and looking through it. "What do you plan to do with this information, Matti?" he said. "I really should burn it."

"I intend to read it to Dan." I held out my hand. It was trembling a little, but it had been a long day. I was still keeping it together. "I'm positive that Willis . . . "

"Asche," Frank said. He was reading it off something in the red file.

"I'm positive he's someone we knew when Dan was in the hospital. I just need to find out one more thing about him and then I'll back off."

I held out my hand again and snapped my fingers. Only once, but I did snap them.

"You're not making sense," Frank said. "If he's someone you know, why didn't you realize it right away when you heard his name?"

That's when I had the melt down. A very brief one. "Because it's complicated," I yelled. "It's . . . just . . . I'm sorry."

Frank lets me get by with a lot, but he does not appreciate being yelled at.

"Please," I said in a soft Bambi's mother's voice. "May I see the newspaper article? I'll give it back."

Frank handed me the folder, but he did not look happy.

"Thank you," I said. I opened it. The clipping was right on top. I decided I was too stressed out to handle reading it myself. I handed it to Dan. "Could you read this out loud?"

Dan looked at the clipping for a minute and then began to read very quietly. "A lightning strike during yesterday's freak electrical storm brought trees down on Highway 6A Sunday afternoon, causing a fatal accident. Killed was passing motorist Willis Asche, 37, and his wife, Selena, also 37."

Dan stopped reading then. "It goes on about the accident. How the car jumped the road and crashed into an embankment."

"But there's more, isn't there?"

Dan studied the clipping, and then looked up at me. His face was suddenly different, pulled down in some way. "Also killed in the accident," he read, "was the couple's six-year-old son, Howard . . . "

He cleared his throat and not for the reason I do it. "Howard Asche. Willis Asche, Jr., nine years old, was the only survivor."

Dan put the clipping in the folder, closed it and laid it back on the desk.

"This sound like your friend?" Frank asked me.

"Yes," I said. "I saw him at the main bus terminal in Kingman one time when he said he was going to visit his family. He had flowers and a small teddy bear with him. The bus he got on went out to a cemetery."

"All the same . . . " Frank said.

"I couldn't find him when I left the hospital," Dan said. "I never told him goodbye."

"I know where he lives," I said.

The next words out of my mouth were for Frank's benefit, because even though he sometimes went too far, I knew he could make things happen.

I was sorry for the meltdown and I used the clearest, calmest voice I could come up with. "Frank," I said, "we have to get back to Metal Springs right away. We have to find Howard."

"Right away," Frank said, "as in tomorrow?"

"Yes," I said. "If we can't go today."

"I've got insurance people coming in the morning, Matti. I can't leave here. And Marsh is expecting a big shipment. You won't be able to pry him away, either."

"You'll find a way though, Dad," I said.

I think it surprised him, me calling him that instead of Frank. But it probably sealed the deal.

4

FLYING

FRANK CAME UP WITH A BRILLIANT solution to our travel problem. Early the next morning Dan and I were on a helicopter to Kingman. One of the X-Treme Ski pilots had to pick up the owner there anyway and we went along.

A friend of Frank's picked us up at the heli-pad south of town and drove us to the main bus terminal. I knew the trip from there to the hospital like the right side of my face.

Except we weren't going to the hospital. We were going to get off at the Metal Springs gas station. I hadn't cleared that with Frank, but I thought it was the best place to look.

We had to be back at the palace by 7:00 PM or he would never allow me to go out alone again until I was eighteen. We'd stay overnight and Frank would drive down to get us sometime the next day. He said he and Dan had some business to take care of before we went back home again, anyway.

It was noisy in the helicopter so Dan and I didn't talk much. I put on my ear muffs and spent my time looking at the way the lake below us cut a long exclamation mark down through the dead trees, and farther south, the living ones. And at the iron hard mountains all around it.

We didn't say much in the car we were picked up in either. Once we got on the bus though and we had a little more privacy, I asked Dan what he thought we should say to Howard.

"If we find him," Dan said. "There's no guarantee we will."

"We'll find him," I said. "What are we going to say to him when we do?"

Dan turned to look at something out the window.

"That appaloosa, again," I thought. "He won't quit." When I looked though, there was just a guy on a tractor driving down the edge of the road.

"Dan?" I said. "About Howard?"

Dan turned back toward me. "He told me when you lose your memory of something it can be very traumatic to get it back. I thought at the time he was saying it for my benefit. Now I think he was talking about himself."

"Maybe," I said.

"What makes you think he'll want to know what his real name is? Or that his family's dead?"

"What makes you think he doesn't know already? Maybe he's just using his brother's name to give him a second chance at being alive."

Dan was quiet for a minute. "All the time I was in the hospital, Howard looked after me. Now . . . "

"I think we'll invite him to come home with us," I said.

Dan laughed. "Frank would have a bird."

"Probably. At first."

"Howard wouldn't come, anyway."

"He told me family was the most important thing in the world. I think he needs one that's above ground." The bus stopped at the Metal Springs gas station.

"What are you doing?" Dan said, when I stood up to get off the bus. "I thought we were going to the hospital."

I shook my head. "This is where Howard lives," I said. "Frank and Marsh and I let him off here once."

Dan grumbled, but he got off after me. Then he stood looking around and shaking his head. "I can't believe he lives here," he said. "Is there even running water in these places? Or heat?"

Metal Springs did look a lot worse than I remembered. Most of the houses had doors or windows missing now. A few had apparently been yanked off their foundations and moved away. There were just holes in the ground where they'd once been.

Gulls picked through the garbage that was everywhere. If you looked hard enough you could probably find a rat.

"Which one of these shacks is he in?" Dan asked finally.

That was the one flaw in my plan. "I don't know exactly," I said. "We're going into the gas station to find out."

5

THAT APPALOOSA AGAIN

THE CASHIER IN THE GAS STATION looked like he was about Dan's age. He was wearing a red bow tie and a vest with a badge pinned on it that said, *Norm*. And under that, *Employee of the Month*.

I pointed to the badge and said, "Congratulations." Frank usually started out that way when he was trying to be friendly and get the other person on his side.

Every now and then, I tried out one of his strategies.

"It's no biggy," Norm said. He had so many freckles on his face and they were so close together in places that he made me think of the Appaloosa I used to see on the way to the hospital.

"I'm the only one who works here now. We're about to close. All these houses are coming down and they're putting in a shopping centre."

"I wonder if you can help us?" I said. Frank's influence coming out in me again. "We're looking for a friend of ours."

"His name is Howard," Dan told him. He gave the usual description. While he was talking it occurred to me that if Howard ever changed his suspenders, we'd have no way of finding him again.

Norm shook his head. "Sorry," he said. "I don't know anyone by that name."

"He lives around here somewhere," I said. "My dad and I dropped him off in front of the gas station a month or so ago."

"Lots of people live in these rundown old houses," Norm said. "They did, anyway."

"So, you're saying you don't know our friend?" Dan asked.

"Not exactly." Norm scratched his neck. "I see him now and then. But," he hesitated, "his name's not Howard."

"How do you know that?" I asked. Or Dan did.

"Why did you want to find this guy again?"

I was beginning to feel impatient so how I answered his question was more my way of handling things than Frank's. "We think he's very ill," I said. "And if we can't find him soon we're going to have to call the doctors at the Metal Springs Hospital and have them send out a search party."

As if that would ever happen.

"You mean he's mental?" Art said.

"We all are. I have T.S. and he has . . . " I pointed at Dan. I didn't know if he actually had something you could name or not. The doctor never told us.

"B.I.N.G.O.," he said. "So does Howard."

"You'd better hope there isn't a full moon tonight," I added.

Norm looked from Dan to me and back again. I could tell we'd worried him. His face was red, where his freckles hadn't blotched together to make it brown. But he wasn't dumb.

"Okay," he said. "Why do you really need to find this guy?"

"Because," Dan told him, and I guess honesty might have been the best way to go in the first place, "he's my friend. I want to make sure he's all right."

"Our friend," I said.

Norm whispered like he thought the gas station might be bugged. "I don't want to get into trouble, but this guy you're talking about? He comes in here once a month to pick up his government check. The owner charges him twenty bucks a month to use this station as his home address."

"You're not the owner?" Dan said.

"You think I'd be wearing this monkey suit if I owned the place?" Norm took off his bow tie and laid it on the counter. "Your guy comes in to get his check like I said. Sometimes I let him use the shower in the back. But I'm telling you, his name's not Howard."

He opened a cupboard behind him and took out a brown envelope with a clear plastic window on the front. He held it out for us to see. A name showed plainly through the window.

Willis Asche, Jr.

"If you can just tell us which of these shacks he lives in," Dan began . . .

" . . . we'll get him and take him home with us." I finished his sentence for him.

Norm shook his head. "I don't know. I really don't. But if you have time to wait, I'm sure he'll be in to pick up this check any minute. It came yesterday. I'm surprised he hasn't been in already."

6

HOWARD

NORM GAVE US TWO PLASTIC CHAIRS to set out on the gravel in front of the gas station. He even offered each of us a free coke and a bag of chips. "On the house," he said. "I feel bad about your friend having to pay to pick up his mail here. He isn't the only one, either. It's just . . . I needed the job."

I appreciated him saying that. After all, he was just another kid trying to make the best of a bad situation.

The wind had come up a bit since we arrived and the sky had that funny look it gets in the fall when it might let down a lot of rain on your head, or it might decide not to. Dan drank his coke fast and then wandered around to the other side of the garage where I couldn't see him.

I thought Howard might be coming on the bus, so I turned my chair toward the highway. While I sat there watching the road I began thinking about what we'd do if Howard actually said yes.

Plan A would be to fix up a place in Cato City, if he insisted on being some place rundown. At least he'd have a great view living there. And we'd be close by.

Plan B involved Frank bringing in another trailer like Dan's for him. Or Howard could even have the egg and Dan could move into the house.

I was so involved with all the possibilities that when I heard Dan calling from the other side of the garage, I had to check out where I was for a minute. Then I got up and ran around to where he was.

"Someone's coming," he said. I looked where he was pointing and saw a figure moving toward us from a little shack off by itself. We stood there and watched as the figure became more Howard-shaped every minute.

"Howard!" Dan called. He waved his arms. I thought Howard saw us but he didn't change his pace.

Dan did, though. He began to jog forward.

"Wait!" I yelled. I put on a burst of speed and caught up with him. I'm supposed to be the greeter, after all. I belong in the front line.

"Howard!" Dan called again.

We both called it out together. "Howard!"

A gust of wind hit us then and it started to rain — not really hard, but not joking around, either. We were all soaked by the time we got together.

It didn't matter, though. As far as I was concerned, all three of us were weatherproof.

Acknowledgements

There are many fine people working in our mental health systems. I appreciate their efforts and in no way do I mean to disrespect the work they do.

Other appreciations go to:

My granddaughter, Erika Jessen, a beautiful young woman of fifteen who is the inspiration for Matti. Erika first learned she had Tourette's when she was in grade three. If I have misrepresented what it's like to live with T. S., the error is entirely mine.

My son Stefan, who has allowed me to write about his experience as a patient in Alberta Hospital when he was eighteen.

Holley Rubinsky, who showed me what it was like to be out on Kootenay Lake in a small boat and helped me get to the other side. She also allowed me to have a close encounter with one of the bears that hung around her house in Kaslo, B.C., in the summer of 2012.

Larry Badry, fire chief and paramedic unit chief of Kaslo, who gave me insight into the multiple hats he wears in his small town.

The people of Gold Hill, Colorado and Slave Lake, Alberta. They survived fires in their communities and were willing to talk about it.

My partner Joseph has lived with me living with this story for four years.

Mary Woodbury in Edmonton and the Mitchells in Columbia Falls, Montana. At various times they loaned me a quiet place to work.

As always, my mentor and friend, Glen Huser.

Thistledown Press for once again seeing value in my manuscript. Without the persistence of small presses like them, many fine books would never be published or read.

Finally, to my editor, R. P. MacIntyre who has an incredible nose for where a story wants to go. Thanks for patience, encouragement and vision. You are the best.

Author's note

The quote beginning, "Hey, Crazyred . . . " is from *Dante's Divine Comedy,* the section called Inferno, Canto XXII, Lines 40-42. Translation by John Ciardi.

Dianne Linden's two previous young adult novels have won critical praise. *Peacekeepers* (2003) was a finalist for Alberta's R. Ross Annett Award for Children's literature in 2004, and the Ontario Library Association's Red Maple Young Reader's Choice Award in 2005. *Shimmerdogs* (2008) was a silver medallist for the Governor General's Award for Children's Literature in that same year and a finalist for the R. Ross Annett Award in 2009. Dianne Linden lives in Edmonton.

Visit Dianne at www.diannelinden.com